MW01133124

# Decked in the Hall

A Finch & Fischer Mystery

J. New

Copyright © J. New 2018

The right of J. New to be identified as the author of this work has been asserted in accordance with the Copyright, Designs and Patents Act 1988.

All rights reserved. No part of this publication may be reproduced, stored in or transmitted into any retrieval system, in any form, or by any means (electronic, mechanical, photocopying, recording or otherwise) without the prior written permission of the publisher. Any person who does any unauthorized act in relation to this publication may be liable to criminal prosecution and civil claims for damages.

This is a work of fiction. Names, characters, businesses, places, events and incidents are either products of the author's imagination or used in a fictitious manner. Any resemblance to actual persons, living or dead, or actual events is purely coincidental.

Cover design copyright © J. New

Cover illustration: WILLIAM WEBB

Cover typography: MARIAH SINCLAIR

## BOOKS BY J. NEW

***The Finch & Fischer Mysteries***

Decked in the Hall

Death at the Duck Pond

Battered to Death

***The Yellow Cottage Vintage Mysteries***

The Yellow Cottage Mystery (FREE)

An Accidental Murder

The Curse of Arundel Hall

A Clerical Error

The Riviera Affair

Full details on these and future books in the series can be found on the website:

**www.jnewwrites.com**

For Annjo & Maisie

For Nikki, Hector & Nero

*'Dogs have a way of finding the people who need them.*
*Filling an emptiness we don't even know we have.'*

– Thom Jones –

# Table of Contents

# One

Everyone in the village of Cherrytree Downs agreed the annual Christmas party in the Village Hall was one of the highlights of the year. The majority of the villagers attended, and with the invite extending to the inhabitants of the five neighbouring villages, a full house was usually guaranteed. In fact, such was the local gossip resulting from a few too many eggnogs, and the abundant bunches of mistletoe hanging from the tinsel festooned ceiling, nothing short of a life or death emergency would keep most people away.

Unfortunately for Penny Finch, her fiancé Edward Marshall wasn't most people. Not that Edward lived in the village, but given their six-year-long engagement, his attendance as her plus-one should have been a given.

"He's what?" Her friend, Susie Hughes, was incredulous. Penny could hear her crunching something at the other end of the telephone line. Depending on whether or not she was on a diet that week, Susie's choice of snack was either crisps or celery sticks. Given that Christmas was only two weeks away, Penny guessed the sound was coming from the former.

"He's double-booked," Penny sighed. "It can't be helped; his accountancy firm's having their Christmas party in a hotel in Winstoke tonight. I thought I'd told you. But never mind, I'll call for you after I've dropped Fischer off with my parents, and we can walk across to the hall together."

Fischer, Penny's Jack Russell terrier, gave an excited yap and spun round twice at the mention of his name, and Penny smiled at his antics.

"Thanks, Penny. That would be great. I know I'm a big girl, but..." Susie's voice cracked. "It's the first time in twenty years I'll be going to the party without James. I'm sure I'll be fine when I get there, but it just brings back memories, you know?"

"Of course, I understand."

Penny had always thought of Susie and James as one of those couples who would be together forever. Childhood sweethearts, from the outside they had appeared to have the perfect life. When the cracks began to show in their relationship, Penny was as surprised as everyone else. But loyal to the end, Susie refused to say a bad word about James, even when the shocking details of his affair had become public knowledge.

"He's the father of my children," she had sniffed to Penny, over many boxes of tissues and glasses of wine in the months after James had moved out. "There's no point making him out to be the villain in all of this. It won't change anything."

Penny, fiercely protective of her friend, had bitten her tongue, even when she bumped into James with his new partner in the supermarket. She had smiled and greeted him through gritted teeth, even though she privately agreed with Susie later that James had downgraded. If perfect couples like Susie and James could split up after fifteen years of marriage and two gorgeous children, what hope did that leave for her and Edward? She pushed the thought out of her head.

"The baby-sitter's arriving at seven," Susie said, sounded chirpier. "I'll be by the door waiting for you at one minute past."

Penny laughed, "In that case, I'd better get a move on. See you later."

Fischer jumped up onto the sofa beside her, eyes bright and his tail wagging furiously. She smiled down at him, "Don't give me that look, Fischer. I'm sorry, but you can't come with me tonight I'm going to a party, and no dogs are allowed."

Fischer hung his head, emitting a soft whine.

Penny, used to his little performances, gently scratched his ears and kissed his little cold nose. "The good news is," she coaxed, "You get to stay with Granny and Granddad, and you know how much they spoil you." She pulled a dog treat from her pocket. "How does that sound?"

Fischer panted in anticipation of his forthcoming treat, and at Penny's command jumped off the sofa and sat in front of her, his tail thumping madly on the rug. With her hands behind her back, Penny shifted the treat to her left hand then held them both out in front of the little dog.

"Where is it then?"

Fischer nudged the left with his nose then set his paw on top and barked once.

"Good boy," Penny said, easing herself up from the squishy cushions as Fischer devoured his snack. Making her way to the fireplace she hunched down, and donning a heat-proof glove opened the wood-burning stove and added several small logs on top of the red and white ash inside. During the winter months, she maintained the cosy temperature in her thatched cottage by having a fire burning all day and much of the night.

A quick check out of the curtained window, confirmed no further snow had fallen since she had returned earlier from helping with the last minute preparations at the Village Hall. Although the thick covering of white outside, which had accumulated over several days, showed no signs of thawing. Whilst the snow added to the festive air on the picturesque village green her house faced onto, it did cause Penny a footwear dilemma for that evening. But if she had to make an appearance wearing wellington boots, she was sure she wouldn't be the only one.

Penny did a quick tidy-up of the living room, arranging several half-read books and magazines into a neat pile on the coffee table. An avid reader, she always had several books on the go. Edward liked to remind her how lucky she was to get paid to talk about literature all day.

"How's my favourite mobile-librarian?" he would ask her, when he telephoned after a busy day in his accountancy firm. Even though she was the only mobile-librarian he knew. "Still keeping the economy afloat with your little green tin of late book fines? I hope you've got them locked safely away." Then he would laugh at his joke, no matter how many times he told it, and never seemed to notice that Penny had stopped laughing with him a long time ago.

Even when Penny tried to explain to him the fines were a point of principle more than a money-making exercise, Edward would still argue the mobile library service was another example of taxpayers' money being wasted.

Penny took the opposite view, "The mobile library's a valuable cultural and social service for the older inhabitants of remote villages. They've limited access to transport to visit the library building in Winstoke, and apart from my visits to see them in the van they might not get to speak to anyone else all day. Don't you think that's a justified taxpayer cost? If anything, it's criminal it's so underfunded."

An ongoing bone of contention between them, they'd decided the best policy was to agree to disagree.

One good thing about Edward not going to the party was that Penny would get a proper chance to speak to her work colleagues, Emma and Sam. They worked at the main library in Winstoke town, along with two other employees who couldn't make it to the dinner this year. Without Edward monopolising her time, Penny was looking forward to discussing all of their latest reads to their heart's content. She hadn't mentioned to Susie that Edward had wanted her to miss the village dinner entirely, in favour of his work Christmas party, but Penny had declined.

"As well as being the fundraiser for the Summer Fete, it's our library work party too," she had told him. "I'm sorry the date doesn't fit in with your plans, but you know the village dinner is always two Saturdays before Christmas."

Edward had let it go at that, although he had forgotten to reimburse her for his ticket which she had purchased months before. But as the event was for a good cause, Penny hadn't given the money another thought. Besides the fact that she was comfortably-off, she didn't want to enter into a conversation with Edward about how his contribution to the Summer Fete would be spent. She was quite happy to leave that up to the committee of capable volunteers in charge of the fundraising efforts. With a club secretary and dedicated bank account, she had no reason to believe things weren't in good hands, especially as the Fete was always spectacular. She suspected Edward was just annoyed he had never been asked to join the Committee as treasurer, even though he'd hinted several times how perfect he would be for the job.

"Well, what do you think?" she asked Fischer when she descended the wooden staircase an hour later, wearing her party best. The dress, a good quality brand she had picked up in the January sales, was several years old but had only been worn a couple of times. Once to her cousin's winter wedding, and the previous year to Edward's office party, where she had received several compliments. Penny stuck to styles that suited her curvy frame without being too revealing, and this was a wrap dress in midnight blue. What she liked most was its simplicity, the only adornment being intricate crystal embellishment on the cuffs. With her dark wavy hair curling on her shoulders and only a touch of makeup on her pale skin, her blue eyes popped in tune with the hue of the dress.

Fischer cocked his head as she checked her reflection in the hallway mirror, and let out a short, sharp bark.

"Thank you, Fischer. I'll take that as a seal of approval."

Selecting her footwear from the row neatly lined up against the wall, Penny carried them back to the staircase and sat on the bottom step. Pulling the khaki wellington boots onto her stockinged feet, she smirked as she straightened up, "Now, that's how to ruin a perfectly good look, Fischer."

She grabbed a pair of heels and stuffed them into a bag, before taking her heavy wool coat off the peg. When she was buttoned up, she wrapped a scarf around her neck and lower face so that only her eyes were visible. She considered a hat, but rejected it on the grounds that her inexpertly, but carefully blow-dried hair would get messed up.

"Time to go, Fischer, fetch your lead," she said, her voice muffled from several layers. Fischer scampered into the kitchen, claws clicking on the floor tiles and returned with his lead in his mouth.

"Clever boy," attaching the lead to his harness Penny lifted her bag and keys from the hall table and opened the door, where a blast of cold air hit her, "Come on then, little man. It's party time."

It was a ten-minute walk by footpath to Penny's parents' house on the edge of village, or five minutes over the village green. Fischer always preferred the route across the green where he had a favourite tree he seemed to gravitate towards. Penny was happy for him to lead her around the duck pond, now almost completely frozen over, and past the brightly-lit Christmas tree in the centre, with a nativity scene laid out at its feet. A snowman with a carrot for a nose and two pieces of coal for eyes had appeared beside the manger, as if in charge of the proceedings. Penny pulled her scarf tighter around her neck. The snowman needed a scarf, but he wasn't having hers.

Strains of Christmas music could be heard coming from the direction of the village hall, and the trail of footprints showed they weren't the first ones heading to the party. Fischer's paws made tiny dots in the snow alongside the outline of Penny's clumpy boots.

"Good evening, Mrs Montague," she said as a white-haired woman tottered past, wearing a fur coat Penny hoped was of the faux variety. "Is Celia not with you tonight?"

Myrtle Montague stopped and squinted at Penny, "Hello, Penelope dear." She smiled at Fischer, who was tugging the lead in an attempt to make a break for his tree. "I'd know that darling dog of yours anywhere. Celia's just parking the Land Rover. I said I'd scoot ahead to get to the bar." She rubbed her leather-gloved hands together with a smile, "I'll have a hot toddy waiting for her by the time she arrives."

"Great idea," Penny said, thinking she couldn't imagine Mrs Montague scooting anywhere. "I won't be far behind you. I'm just taking Fischer to stay with my parents."

"Jolly good," the old lady nodded. "See you shortly then, Penelope."

Mrs Montague lived with her housekeeper, Celia, in a grand old house on one of the rolling hills overlooking Cherrytree Downs, and was one of Penny's regular library customers. She often arrived at the end of the lane, where Penny parked the library van, with a bag of homemade biscuits for Penny and a treat for Fisher, and she was never known to pass anyone without a good word.

Penny waited to make sure Mrs Montague got across the road without mishap then let Fischer drag her to his tree, where, barely visible, he snuffled in the deep snow for a while before taking care of business. The streets were devoid of traffic and the snow was thick and crunchy, rather than being too slippery. That would come in the morning, after icy surfaces had formed overnight.

Not wanting to let the heat out, only her father's eyes

were visible peering around the door after she rang the bell of her parent's home several minutes later.

"There you are, at last. Your mum's been waiting for Fischer. She's cooked kidneys especially for him."

"I think he knows that," Penny said, handing her father Fischer's lead, which she'd just unclipped, while the small dog nudged the bottom of the door, then shot inside over Albert Finch's size ten feet in an attempt to get to where the delicious smells were coming from. "I won't come in, Dad, or I'll be late to Susie's. I'll see you in the morning."

"As you like, Penny," said the voice behind the door. "I expect Fischer will have learned a new trick by tomorrow if your mother's got anything to do with it."

"Well, as long as it's not how to open the fridge door. He's already smarter than any dog I know and he's only six months old. Now go back inside before you get cold."

Susie was already standing on her doorstep waiting when she got there. Penny thought her friend looked thin, despite her protestations that she had been overindulging in Christmas goodies since Halloween. She hoped Susie wouldn't be joining the January class at the local slimming club, as was her custom. The Heartbreak Diet seemed to have done the job already.

"Nice boots," Susie said, eyeing Penny's wellies. "It's not a barn dance, you know."

"Very funny. I don't care what I look like. I've no intention of falling and breaking something. Besides desert boots are hardly this year's festive look."

Susie laughed, "Yes, well I don't want to break anything either. Come on Cinders let's get to this ball and have some fun."

The sound of the music from the hall was getting louder as they approached and Susie grinned, "They're playing that old Christmas CD again. The one with all the cheesy hits. Don't you just love it?"

Penny matched her smile with one of her own. Seeing Susie's eyes light up, even if only for a moment, was a positive step. They stopped outside the hall. Fairy lights were strung across the doorway, and a bunch of balloons tied to the sign blew in the wind.

Penny opened her bag, "Let me lean on you while I change my shoes, then you can do the same," she said, trying to step into her heels without getting her feet wet. She failed, but it didn't dampen her mood. Having hung up their coats and scarves on the pegs at the door they were finally ready. "Shall we?"

Penny and Susie walked into a time warp. It was a repeat of every village Christmas party they had ever attended, and there had been many. The same decorations made an appearance every year. A multitude of different-sized tables, dressed in white paper tablecloths and festive plastic overlays, displayed gilt crackers on every place setting. No detail had been missed, right down to three different picnic glasses per person, Father Christmas serviettes and party streamers everywhere.

Penny checked the seating plan on the board at the entrance, "I'm on Table Three with Emma and Sam from the library, Mr Kelly and the Evans contingent." Mr and Mrs Evans owned the bakery in the village and were known for the best scones in the whole of Hantchester county. Their daughter, Stella, was younger than Penny, but Penny knew her well. "And Lloyd Masterson," she added with a grimace. "Oh, well."

"I'm at Table Five with my colleagues from the Winstoke Gazette." Susie adjusted her glasses and peered closer, "Oh no, and the Wargraves. No doubt I'll have to listen to Julia's many petty complaints, like how her emptied wheelie bin is always left a foot further from her gate than she likes, or how The Gazette's photographer never gets her good side. Not to mention her superior knowledge of gardening. She doesn't even drink, unless she spikes that bottle of cordial she carries around with her everywhere."

"I've wondered about that too, although you can have a good time without drinking you know."

Julia Wargraves was famous for winning the annual Best Kept Garden competition every year since its inception. She and her husband were known to celebrate her victories in style, usually ending up with a party in the local pub, the Pig and Fiddle, where Julia was in her element holding court among the village natives.

"Well it can't be helped, I'll try and be nice. Season of goodwill and all that. But if you need rescuing from that pompous Lloyd Masterson, just let me know," Susie whispered to Penny as they made their way to their respective tables. "I bet he wants to pull your cracker."

Penny gave Susie a withering look, "I'm quite capable of looking after myself, thank you. And please, no more bad jokes." She let out a half-laugh, "That's Edward's domain."

Lloyd Masterson cornered her as soon as she sat down. "Is Edward not here tonight?" He asked, moving into the chair beside her, even though it had been designated for someone else. "Never mind I'm happy to keep you company, my dear."

Penny's eyes glazed over as Lloyd launched into a monologue concerning return policies for published books. He owned the bookshop and tearoom in Winstoke that had previously belonged to Penny's parents before they retired. For some reason he seemed to think the connection made him and Penny friends for life. Normally, anything to do with books was Penny's favourite subject, but where Lloyd was concerned the less said the better, if only to end the conversation as quickly as possible. She gave an animated wave to her colleagues Emma and Sam who were approaching the table just in time to rescue her.

Much more to Penny's liking was the old gentleman, Mr Kelly, seated on her other side. The retired head teacher of the local primary school, he was intelligent, witty and shared Penny's love for mystery books. Once the Evans' arrived and the wine started flowing, the lively chatter from the rest of the group made up for Lloyd's interminable droning.

"What on earth is that?" Lloyd waved his knife at Penny's plate when they returned from the buffet table.

"It's a Portobello pot roast, with three cheese mashed potato and roasted garlic and kale stuffing," Penny said. "I'm a vegetarian."

"Shame," Lloyd said, tucking into his turkey and ham dinner with gusto.

"Not at all," Penny assured him, tasting her meal. "This is delicious."

Mr Evans declared the Pig and Fiddle had surpassed themselves at this year's catering, and everyone raised their glass in toast as Mrs Duke, one of the village volunteers for the evening, started to clear the table. By the time the bowls of Christmas pudding and trifle had been scraped clean, the band playing cover songs had warmed up and the party proper commenced. Penny was contemplating whether or not to have cheese and crackers when she spotted Susie sitting alone at her table nearby.

"Sorry, Lloyd," Penny said, when he asked her to dance. "I'm going to sit this one out. I just need to check if Susie's all right. You don't mind, do you?"

He shook his head, looking around for another victim. While his head was turned, Penny slipped away and sat down beside Susie, who was nursing a cup of coffee. "Hey, are you all right?"

Susie nodded, "Yes. I'm fine. I was in danger of getting tearful, so I ditched the wine. You?"

"Same. Not tearful, but the effort of drowning out Lloyd

was exhausting." Her eyes followed Susie's across the dance floor, and her mouth fell open. "Gosh, look at Mr Kelly spinning Celia around like that. Who knew he had it in him?"

Susie smiled, "The older generation really know how to dance properly. My mum and dad won several local competitions for jiving. Pity we didn't learn those sort of moves in the eighties." Her gaze turned to a corner of the dance floor, where a cluster of people were gathered around. "What's going on over there? It looks like someone has fallen."

It was hard to decipher over the music, but Penny heard a shout, and a man came running across the dance floor to the head table to speak to one of the organisers. The harried look on his face told her something was terribly wrong. "I think there's been an accident," she said, springing up. A trained first aider, her immediate reaction was to go and help. She rushed across the room just as the music came to an abrupt stop and the main lights came on. A hush fell over the proceedings.

"Excuse me, First Aider coming through," Penny said, making her way into the huddle. Julia Wargraves was lying sprawled out on the floor, unconscious. Penny kneeled down and pressed two fingers to the side of Julia's neck, then did the same with her wrist. Julia's skin was still warm, her face tinged pink, but there was no pulse. No heartbeat. Nothing. "Call an ambulance," she demanded of the person standing nearest to her, and rolled up her sleeves.

Someone beat her to it, "Let me," said a voice beside her, and a man crouched down. She recognised him as Vincent Adams, a St John's Ambulance volunteer from Rowan Downs, the next village along. Penny leaned in closer to Julia, willing her to breathe, which is when she detected a very faint smell of bitter almonds and immediately alarm bells rang in her mind. She urged Vincent to provide hands-only CPR, and while he was surprised he did as she asked, recognising the urgency in her voice.

Vincent kept up the CPR until the paramedics arrived, but the emergency response team shook their heads. "I'm sorry. She's gone," one of them said, ushering the crowd away.

Penny could see that Vincent, head bowed, was visibly shaken. She tried to reassure him, "Vincent, it wasn't your fault. You did everything you could, but it was already too late."

He nodded, glancing back at Julia's body. "Must have been a heart attack. A big one, to go that quick."

Acting on instinct, Penny whispered, "Did you smell the almonds?" She thought Vincent gave her a strange look, but maybe she was imagining it.

"There's marzipan in the Christmas cake, Penny. Not to mention the almond cake," he said, patting her shoulder as if she was going mad. But she wasn't, she was certain of it.

Penny rushed back to Susie, "Julia Wargraves is dead. And I think she was murdered."

# Two

Looking around the table for clues Penny carefully lifted Julia's bottle of cordial. A few remnants of food remained on the table, and she crammed all of it onto a plate. "Did you see anything? Think, Susie, think."

Susie shook her head in shock, "No, not a thing. She seemed fine before she started dancing." She hesitated before continuing, "Penny, are you sure you're not overreacting? I know people get murdered in village halls in those mystery books you like to read, but it doesn't happen in real life."

"Don't be so sure of that," Penny said. She pushed the plate of food and the bottle of cordial across the table, so they were in front of Susie. "Don't let anyone touch these, okay? They might be needed as evidence. Wait there. I'm going to get our coats and boots."

The mood in the Village Hall was sombre as the guests filed their way outside. Penny spotted Mr Kelly standing by the door and touched his arm on her way past, "Are you all right getting home, Mr Kelly?"

He nodded, "Yes, thank you, Penny. My daughter is coming from Chiddingborne to pick me up. I expect it will take her a little longer than usual in this weather though."

Susie stepped beside them holding the cordial bottle in one hand and the plate of food, now covered in a plastic film, in the other. "We can wait with you, if you'd like?"

"Absolutely not. You two ladies run along." He gave them a tight smile, "Terrible end to what was a lovely evening isn't it? But it's Stanley Wargraves we should be worried about, not me."

Penny glanced over her shoulder. Stanley Wargraves, normally a jovial fellow with a permanently red face, which was perfect for his role as Father Christmas on carol singing evening, was being comforted by one of his Estate Agency employees. There was no trace of his jolly manner to be seen now. He held his head in his hands, looking up now and then, eyes bright with pain and unshed tears, in the direction of the of the dance floor where his wife lay dead. In his fifties, he was at least ten years younger than Mr Kelly, but seemed to have aged decades in the last fifteen minutes.

An icy blast of air hit Penny's face from the open hall door as she turned back to Mr Kelly, "You're right. Poor Stanley's in a bad way, I can't imagine what he must be feeling. Such a tragedy. But at least he has some support. Goodnight, Mr Kelly."

"Goodnight, girls. Mind how you go in the snow."

Penny and Susie walked down the steps of the hall in silence.

"What now?" Susie asked.

A group of revellers passed them heading in the direction of The Pig & Fiddle, keen to continue the party somewhere warm that served alcohol.

"I couldn't face going to the pub," Penny said. "It doesn't seem right to continue partying."

"I know what you mean. How about we go to mine and have a cup of tea?"

"We really should stop this rock and roll lifestyle you know."

Susie laughed, "Come on, at least the baby-sitter will be glad to get away early."

Susie's children, aged ten and thirteen, were no longer babies, although Susie, mostly in jest, said their behaviour occasionally indicated otherwise. They walked at a brisk pace, snow crunching underfoot, to Susie's house, a Victorian red-brick terrace. Inside, a wall of heat greeted them, and Penny warmed her hands by the fire while Susie paid the baby-sitter.

"Are you sure you want tea?" Susie said, when she returned. "I've got something stronger, if you prefer?"

Penny shook her head, "It's perfect. You know me, I can never refuse a good cup of tea." Penny had been a tea collector for years, and while she was not keen on red berry or traditional fruit teas, she adored Rooibos, the red tea from South Africa, especially if it was infused with cinnamon. She also loved the eastern varieties, as well as a recently discovered apple, cinnamon and raisin blend, which was very much to her taste. She'd always found tea wonderfully calming, and after the shock of Julia Wargrave's death it was exactly what she needed.

"I'll put the kettle on."

Penny could hear Susie rattling about in the kitchen. Her friend kept a tin stocked with a selection of tea bags especially for Penny's visits. Sometimes, Susie gave Penny a choice of tea, and other times it was pot luck. Penny knew it was definitely a pot luck sort of a night. Being picky about Ceylon versus Assam seemed trivial considering the events of the evening.

Susie appeared with a fully-laden tray, which wobbled ever so slightly as she carried it over to the coffee table. There were two small teapots, bone china mugs, milk and sugar and a plate of chocolate biscuits wrapped in festive metallic foil. Penny recognised the biscuits as the kind only available in boxes at Christmas and sold at extortionate prices.

"Regular for me, and fancy stuff for you," Susie said, setting down the tray, and pointing out which teapot was which. Penny lifted the lid and stirred hers, inhaling the scent of Rooibos and Cinnamon. She sat back and let it infuse before pouring.

Susie loaded her mug with tea, milk and two teaspoons of sugar. Seeing Penny watching her, she added an extra half teaspoon of sugar, "Don't give me that look," Susie said, taking a sip. "Sweet, milky tea does it for me every time. I'm a cheap date." Her expression faltered, "Not that I'll be dating any time soon."

"I know it's early days," Penny said. "But at some point, you'll feel differently. There's plenty of time for that in the future though. For now, you just need to concentrate on looking after yourself and the children. I think you're doing a wonderful job so far, by the way. I can only imagine how hard it must be."

Susie unwrapped a biscuit, rolling its foil into a tiny ball and setting it onto the tray. "I'm holding it together by a thread," she said, before taking a bite. Crumbs fell as she continued, her chin wobbling. "James wants a divorce. The solicitor's letter arrived on Tuesday."

"Oh." Penny knew Susie had been hoping for a reconciliation and had urged her errant husband to attend marriage counselling with her, despite his insistence he had moved on. "I'm sorry, Susie. That seems so…final."

"Yes," Susie swallowed. "But that's not the worst of it. We're going to have to sell the house. I haven't told the kids yet." She set her half-eaten biscuit down on the table and stared at Penny. "Chocolate and sweet, milky tea are my way of papering over the cracks. What I really want, is to cry and scream and roar from a cliff top where no one can hear me, and for this nightmare to be over. I'm dreading what the new year will bring, Penny. I wake up every day feeling fine for about two seconds until the gnawing in my stomach kicks in and I remember why."

Penny remembered carrying that same sick feeling around many years before, after university when she split from her first real boyfriend. A man she thought she was going to marry. She had retreated to Cherrytree Downs to lick her wounds, allowing herself time to recover slowly with the help of her parents and Susie. If there was any way she could repay Susie with only a fraction of the kindness and support her friend had shown her over the years, she was happy to do so.

"Susie, I know how much you love this house. I have a little money put by. If you..."

Susie held up her hand, "No I can't do that, Penny, but I really appreciate the offer, thank you. I'm meeting a financial adviser next week to see if I can afford to buy James out. But after a ten-year career break and considering what my crummy job at The Gazette pays, I'm not holding my breath."

"Any chance of a pay rise?"

"No, I already asked. My salary review's not for another six months. Until I get promoted to Junior Reporter, I'm stuck at the bottom of the ladder for a while yet."

Penny took a sip of her tea. "Hmm. Well, at least the only way is up. Anyway, the offer's there if you change your mind."

Susie nodded, "I know. Thanks, but I'll manage. Some people have it a lot worse. Stanley Wargraves, for one."

The image of Stanley being comforted as they were leaving the village hall flashed through Penny's mind. She frowned, "Did you notice the woman fussing over Stanley? I thought she seemed overly-familiar with him, or am I being harsh?"

"That was Ruth Lacey, his secretary. It's hard to say what's appropriate in the circumstances, don't you think? Secretaries always fuss over their bosses, it's part of the job description. And I'm sure her husband Mark was around somewhere. I think Ruth and Mark were sitting at Mrs Montague's table."

"You're right, I'm probably reading too much into it." All the same, Penny filed it away for future reference. She didn't know Ruth apart from to nod hello to on the rare occasion when they passed in the street, and she hadn't recognised her that evening. But Edward knew Mark Lacey through work. Or, maybe it was from the Cricket Club. Either way, the two men were on friendly terms.

"What are you going to do with the food and drink you took from the hall?" Susie asked, nodding toward the plate and bottle Penny had left on the dining table.

Penny followed her gaze, "I suppose I should hand them into the police, and they can get them analysed or something." Turning back to Susie, she added, "Perhaps it will turn out to be nothing and Julia did die of natural causes, but I'd rather be certain even if I end up looking stupid. I'd never forgive myself if her death was foul play and whoever was responsible got away with it."

"No one would ever think you're stupid, Penny. Quite the opposite. You know what I think?"

"No," Penny smiled. "But I'm sure you're going to tell me."

"It's nice of you to care. For most of the villagers, Julia dropping dead like that is just something to talk about in The Pig and Fiddle for the next few days. Then, it will all blow over and the local gossips will find something else to talk about. Meanwhile, Julia will be six feet under and no one will give her another thought, apart from poor Stanley as he grieves. I know Julia wasn't the easiest of people to get along with, but if her death was suspicious then she at least deserves someone decent to look into it."

If Penny had any doubts before that what she was doing was the right thing, Susie's input strengthened her resolve.

"I'll walk over to the police house in the morning."

"I've heard PC Bolton has been on a go-slow ever since he announced he's retiring next year," Susie said. "Although, I'm not sure how he could get much slower than he already was. But are you sure a local village bobby is the right person to give this stuff too? He's the last of a dying breed, and between you and me, word at the paper is once he retires we'll no longer have a village PC due to cutbacks. Personally, I think you'd be better off going to the main station in Winstoke. Humphrey Bolton is great for keeping the peace in the villages, finding stolen bikes and rescuing cats from trees, but if this is murder like you think, he'll be way out of his depth."

"Yes, you're right. He'd probably just pass it onto Winstoke anyway so I'll just be saving him the job. The van has winter tyres, so the snow won't be a problem."

Penny's mobile library was a converted VW Camper-van. She owned it herself and the council paid her an allowance for wear and tear and mileage relating to her work for the library service. The rest of the time she was free to use it for her own purposes. Sadly, it was no longer suitable for camping, she could hardly try and squeeze her size fourteen figure into a sleeping bag on a bookshelf. Just then the living room door creaked open, and a small figure dressed in pink pyjamas and trailing a blanket wandered into the room.

"Hey, sweetheart, what are you doing up?" Susie stretched out her arms as her ten-year-old daughter, Ellen, approached the sofa, and enveloped her up in a hug. After a few moments, Ellen pulled away, "Can I sleep in your bed tonight, Mummy?" she asked Susie with pleading eyes. "I'm scared."

"Of course you can, darling," Susie motioned to Penny that she would be right back, then got up and steered Ellen out of the room.

By the time Susie returned, Penny had finished her tea and was ready to leave. "I'll get going, Susie. You've got your hands full."

"Here, let me put those in a bag," Susie said, taking the wrapped plate of food and bottle of cordial out of Penny's hands. Penny followed her into the galley kitchen in the rear of the house, where Susie found a carrier bag. She handed it back to Penny with a hollow expression.

"Ellen's started wetting the bed," she said, holding back tears. Her voice was a whisper, "And Billy's sworn off football practice because his dad's one of the coaches. I don't know what to do."

"Ssh," Penny said, stroking Susie's back. "We'll work it out, Susie. I know it's easier said than done, but try not to worry. They just need time to adjust, you all do. And remember I'm here whenever you need me."

Susie walked Penny to the door, wiping a tear from her cheek, "Let me know how you get on tomorrow with the food and the cordial, will you? Maybe you could keep some back, because if it's contaminated I might need it for James."

Penny knew she wasn't serious, Susie didn't have a mean bone in her body, but the fact that she felt able to joke at all was a relief.

# THREE

Penny removed her wellies in the hallway of her parents' cottage and followed her mother into the kitchen. Fischer hurtled from his food bowl to greet her, jumping up with excited little yips and his tail wagging so fast it was practically a blur. Penny crouched down and scooped him up in a hug and was rewarded with a full face and ear wash.

"Now that's what a call a greeting! How's my little fish face?" she said, carrying him to the table and gently lowering him back to earth. "I hope you were a good boy?"

"Of course, he was," her father said from his seat at the head of the old pine table, where the Sunday newspaper was spread out just so. The Sunday edition contained a lot of sections, and Albert liked to read them in a certain order. He started with the books and finished up with finance, with news, gardening and travel somewhere in between. The style section was pushed to one side, for his wife Sheila's perusal. She usually got around to looking at it by Tuesday, or sometimes not at all. "He knows we don't take any nonsense, do we Fischer? We don't spoil him like you do."

Penny caught her mother's eye and smiled. They both knew about the treats Albert gave Fischer when he thought no one was looking, and the fact he would quite willingly give up his favourite chair in the sitting room if he found the little dog already using it. Her father wasn't half as stern as he made himself out to be.

Her mother pulled out a chair and set down a small teapot and cup. "Sit down and tell us about the party, Penny. We heard there was quite a stir."

"There was indeed. Julia Wargraves collapsed and was pronounced dead at the scene. Everyone had to leave. It was awful, seeing her husband so upset like that. I'm sure he was in shock."

Her father lowered the newspaper. "Being married to Julia can't have been easy. Maybe he's had a..."

Sheila tutted and interrupted before he could finish his sentence, "Bite your tongue, Albert Finch. Julia may not have been the most popular woman in the village, but I'm sure Stanley loved her, and she worked hard in that garden. It was always beautiful, you'll have to give her that."

"True," Albert conceded. "But I won't mention anything about pushing up daisies."

Penny groaned. Her father had a somewhat warped sense of humour and said what he thought, even if some of the jokes he came out with were a bit controversial.

"I heard Vincent Adams tried his hardest, but there was no saving her," Sheila murmured. "Such a young woman to have a heart attack like that. Only in her early fifties."

"It's amazing what you can find out on a trip to the newsagent, isn't it, Fischer?" Penny stroked the bundle of white and brown fur that had once again landed on her lap. Looking across at her mother she added, "I don't think it was a heart attack."

"Perhaps a massive stroke?" Albert offered.

"No, Dad. I think Julia was murdered."

"Really?" Albert adjusted his reading glasses while he considered what Penny had said. "Why do you think so, my dear?"

Penny knew her father would never dismiss any opinion of hers out of hand. If Penny told him she had seen a spaceship and little grey aliens in the garden, she knew he would humour her, at least until he had heard the evidence.

"Her breath smelled of bitter almonds," Penny said. "I was right beside the body when Vincent was trying to revive her. It was unmistakable. That's why I told him to do hands-only CPR otherwise he might have been badly affected."

Albert's eyes widened, "That's very interesting. What are you going to do?"

"I took some food from Julia's table, just in case it was poisoned," Penny said. "And the bottle of cordial she carried everywhere. I'm going to hand it in to the police and be done with it. If it turns out to be nothing, so be it. At least my conscience will be clear."

"It's certainly better to err on the side of caution, don't you agree, Sheila? I wish I'd thought of that before eating the coleslaw you brought from town the other day. My constitution's not been the same since."

"Don't blame me, Albert, you know coleslaw doesn't agree with you." Sheila smiled, "Penny, will you stay for lunch?"

"I can't, Mum. I'm meeting Edward in Chiddingborne to visit the Christmas market. It's nice to have a walk around, and we can have lunch and pick up some last-minute gifts at the same time." She checked her watch, "Actually, Fischer and I had best be off if we're stopping at the police station in Winstoke on the way." Fischer's ears pricked up at the mention of his name, and he jumped off Penny's lap and made his way to the door. Penny got up from the table.

"Do you mind if I make a suggestion?" Albert said.

"Of course not, Dad. What's on your mind?"

"There's bound to be an autopsy, they have to with sudden deaths, a death certificate won't be issued otherwise. Why not wait and see what the coroner's report says? If there's any suspicion regarding her death, you can hand the food and drink in then. It might save you wasting your afternoon, not to mention wasting police time."

"I hadn't thought of that. Good idea, Dad. Thanks." Penny took the lead from the table and called Fischer to come back, then bent down to attach it to his harness. "Not that I'm really worried about it, but it might save face as well if I'm wrong."

"Before you go, Penny, I wanted to ask you about Christmas Day," her mother said. "Will you and Fischer be coming here? Edward's also welcome, if he'd like."

"Of course, Mum." Penny grinned. "Me and Fischer wouldn't miss it for the world, it's my little guy's first Christmas! Right, Fischer?" the little dog barked in agreement. "I'm not sure about Edward, though I'll have to check with him, but as you know he usually visits his own family for a few days, so I think you can safely count him out."

Albert muttered something under his breath.

"What was that, Dad?"

"Nothing, dear," her father smiled.

"In that case," Sheila said, "do you think Susie and her children would like to join us? There's plenty of room, and her children adore Fischer. That son of hers is such a kind young man. I saw him helping Mrs Montague with her shopping bags the other day. He made two trips from the greengrocer's to her car."

Penny's face lit up, "That's a great idea, I'll ask her. She said she's dreading Christmas without James there, so she'll probably be glad of a change of scene. That's really thoughtful, thanks, Mum."

"It was your dad's idea."

Penny watched while Albert buried his face in the newspaper, "Thanks, Dad."

Her heart was warmed by them both. An only child, she had grown up enveloped in the steadfast love they had for her as well as for each other. She really was very lucky. "Don't get up, Mum, I'll see myself out. Come on then, Fischer, it's off to market we go. There might be sausages!"

What Penny loved most about the Christmas Market at Chiddingborne was that it had retained its local character, and hadn't become one of the tacky affairs she had come across in larger towns in recent years. For six weeks every year Chiddingborne Green was transformed into a festive winter wonderland, which would have done the North Pole proud. Artisan food, one-of-a-kind gifts from independent sellers and craft beer tents had won out over the mass-produced Christmas tat, and drunken crowds she had witnessed at other events.

Delicious aromas of Cinnamon, eggnog, hot chocolate and roasting chestnuts vied for attention, and Penny took a deep breath savouring it all, she loved Christmas time.

She and Edward meandered along the circular path connecting the individual wooden chalets strung with multi coloured fairy lights, admiring their wares. While Fischer had his nose to the ground following a multitude of tantalising smells. Every now and then Penny would stop to buy something, mentally ticking off her gift list in her head. A pot of blackberry jam or a bag of fudge for work colleagues, a musical jewellery box for Susie's daughter, Ellen, and a knitted tea cosy for herself. Along with Penny's tea collection, she was the proud owner of an array of novelty teapots in a multitude of designs, ranging from little houses and shops to her favourite, The Mad hatter's Tea Party. She also had several tea cosies to keep them warm.

"Let me buy you that," Edward said, after she had agonised over which design to choose, and opted for one that looked like a Christmas pudding. "I haven't bought your present yet."

Penny watched his expression change when he saw the price tag. He looked at her in surprise, "Fifteen pounds? Maybe not, then. This must be someone's idea of a joke."

"It's handcrafted and beautifully made," Penny pointed out. "Considering the time and materials to make it, I don't think that's unreasonable at all." She gave the woman who owned the stall an apologetic smile. "And," she finished, looking up at Edward, "I really like it."

Edward frowned, and walked away. That was his way of saying the conversation was over.

"I'll take it." Penny smiled at the woman and took the cash out of her purse. She wasn't one for throwing money around any more than Edward was, but she valued quality, as well as supporting the whole ethos behind the market. If people like her didn't buy anything, then next year they were likely to be faced with stalls of mass-produced imports from China. While the woman wrapped her purchase, Penny lifted a few business cards from the table, to leave on the counter in the library.

She and Fischer caught up with Edward beside a stall selling original wooden clogs with upturned toes. "Thistle Grange village clogs?" Edward said incredulously, lifting one up and turning it over in his hand. He shook his head, muttering something under his breath.

Penny reached for the clog and set it back down among the display. She decided to come back alone and buy her Christmas tree later that week. She had a feeling if Edward learned the price of the spruce trees from Oaklands Farm, who always had a pitch at the market, the afternoon might be ruined.

"I haven't got your present yet either," she said brightly, wondering if she should suggest something different this year. She thought a joint present would be nice, like an activity or experience they could do together. Wine-tasting, perhaps, or a day trip somewhere.

"But you always get me tickets for the annual vintage Mini show," Edward said with a frown.

"I know, but maybe it's time for a change?" It wasn't even as if Penny went to the show with Edward. He preferred to take his brother, Eric, despite the fact he expected Penny to attend numerous other Mini events with him between May and September.

"I don't like surprises."

"You realise you sound like a sulky child?" She glanced across at his set jaw and sighed. "Mini show tickets it is, then." There was no point mentioning the cost was a lot more than fifteen pounds. That would just be petty.

They continued the round of stalls in silence, with numerous vendors and customers alike stopping them to pet the wiggling puppy, who greeted every stranger as though they were a friend.

"Did you have to bring the dog, Penny? It's taking twice as long as it normally would to get round the market."

Penny glared at Edward, "Yes I did. Where I go, Fischer goes, he's family. Besides I didn't realise we were in a rush." She bent down and gave the little dog a hug, whispering in his ear, "Just ignore him, Fischer." He gazed at her with big brown eyes the colour of melted chocolate and licked her nose.

"Oh look, there's Mark Lacey," Edward said, steering her across to a stall with a long queue, selling hand-pressed cordials and juices. "We'd better say hello."

Penny saw someone else she recognised, "Hello, Mrs Duke," she said to the woman who had just been served and was walking away. Mrs Duke gave her a nod and made her way to a pet stall, where she stared at the numerous cat toys before scuttling off.

Penny realised someone was speaking to her. "Sorry," she said, addressing Ruth Lacey, who was smiling in her direction. Edward and Mark were already deep in conversation. "I was miles away. I'm very sorry about what happened to Julia Wargraves last night. How is Stanley bearing up?"

Ruth, hands stuffed in the pockets of her wax jacket,

shivered. "Devastated, naturally, and probably still in shock. I called on him this morning to check he had eaten and he wasn't himself at all. Of course, we'll all rally around and do what we can to help but getting through the next few days is going to be tough for him."

"Well, I imagine that's just the beginning," Penny said. "They say the loneliness gets worse and reality sinks in when people stop calling. Stanley and Julia didn't have any children, did they?"

Ruth shook her head. "No children. They..." She checked herself. "Never mind."

"Does Stanley know yet what the cause of death was?" Penny hoped she sounded casual. She bent down to pat Fischer so Ruth wouldn't see her face. "Julia seemed so fit and healthy, but then I suppose you never really know." She straightened up, eager to gauge Ruth's reaction. She couldn't be sure, but she thought Ruth's expression flickered.

"I'm not sure." Ruth shifted her weight from foot to foot, avoiding catching Penny's eye. "Mark," she said, tugging at her husband's sleeve. "I think we'd better go, sweetheart. It's getting late."

Mark reached an arm around Ruth and pulled her close, kissing her temple. She leaned into his shoulder. "I thought you wanted to buy some of the apple and ginger cordial you love so much."

"It doesn't matter. The queue's too long," she said.

"I'm sure there's some at home anyway," Mark said. He

beamed across at Penny. "Happy Christmas, Penny, if I don't see you before."

"Thanks, Mark, you too. Bye, Ruth." Penny watched them walk off, Ruth clinging to Mark like a limpet.

Edward looked at his watch. "Late?" he said. "I don't know what she's talking about, it's only two o'clock. Come on I'll treat you to lunch. As long as it's not too expensive."

Penny nodded, "I thought you'd never ask."

# Four

Penny used a plastic ice scraper to clear the overnight fall of snow from mobile library's windscreen. Leaving the engine running and the heater on, she trudged back inside to pick up her lunch; a Thermos flask of carrot and coriander soup and the crusty bread she had prepared the night before. She tried to be organised and plan meals in advance each weekend for the upcoming week, but failing that there was usually something in the freezer she could use as a backup for her evening meal. For winter lunches, homemade soup was a mainstay she didn't think she could survive without, and she made a batch in the slow cooker without fail every Sunday.

She added a handful of dog treats to her bag then went to the hall where Fisher was eagerly waiting, his tail wagging and his paws doing a little tap-dance in his impatience to be off.

"I wished I felt as bright eyed and bushy tailed as you on a Monday morning, Fischer," she said, checking she had everything she needed for the day. She lifted her keys from a brightly glazed bowl on the hall table, which was Fischer's cue to make a bolt for the door and dash out as soon as she opened it. Although she had cleared the front pathway of snow earlier and was wearing her wellies, she was still much slower than Fischer making her way back to the van. Mrs Todd, her neighbour who lived next door but one, had slipped on the ice and broken her arm just a few days before. Penny wasn't about to make the same mistake.

The van was toasty warm, and the windscreen had defrosted when she climbed back in, Fischer riding shotgun in the passenger seat. One of the advantages of owning the van was for all intents and purposes, she made her own rules. Whilst no one from Hantchester Borough Council, the governing authority for the Winstoke library, had said Fischer was allowed in the van during working hours, no one had said he wasn't either.

It was a busy time of morning in Cherrytree Downs, with schoolchildren wrapped up in a colourful array of woolly scarves, gloves and hats, walking to the local primary school on High Lane. The younger children, accompanied by their parents, watched in envy while the bigger ones threw snowballs and skidded along the footpath. Penny adjusted her driver's mirror and looked sideways at Fischer, who was sniffing and pawing at the window, watching the fun unfold outside.

"Sorry little man, we can't go and join in I'm afraid," she said with a smile. "You and I have work to do. Oops, I forgot the lights." Penny reached behind her and flipped a switch attached to a battery pack. The multi-coloured Christmas lights strung around the van began to twinkle.

"That's better," Penny said. "Now, for some music." Pressing the button on the dashboard to turn on the CD player, strains of a classic Christmas hit filled the air. Nodding her head to the beat and feeling a lot more festive than she had when she woke, she set off for her first pitch of the day.

As well as serving the village of Cherrytree Downs, the mobile library was responsible for covering the other five local villages and hamlets which made up the district of Hampsworthy Downs. Every week, her route was the same, and Monday morning saw her and Fischer heading to Rowan Downs, two miles from home. The journey took them up past the highest point on the downs, Sugar Hill, from where the twisting road meandered down again into the village. Penny had the route planned like that, the first stop of the week also being the quietest, with only a handful of people turning up to exchange their books. As the days wore on, the stops got busier, and sometimes Penny had to restock the van at the main Winstoke library before she finished for the week on Thursday at five o' clock. She had volunteered to reduce her hours to four days a week when the Council was making cuts the previous year, and had found she loved her three-day weekends so much that she confessed to Susie she wished she had done it years earlier.

The morning passed without event, and Penny took advantage of the lull between the handful of library customers to add a few finishing touches to the van's Christmas decorations.

"Let's see what we've got left in here," she said to Fischer, pulling a cardboard box out of a small storage cupboard that had been part of the original camper van.

"Hmm." There was a string of tinsel, a Christmas tree fairy, a red reindeer nose and a sprig of plastic mistletoe. The reindeer nose was put to good use on the front of the van, the tinsel around the steering wheel and the fairy on the dashboard. Fischer stared at the mistletoe, whining when Penny placed it back in the box. She looked across at him, shaking her head.

"We have to hide that, after what happened last year. Mr Atkins got a bit carried away and Mrs Potter complained. She said she got quite a fright, although between you and me, I think she was secretly flattered."

Stowing the box back in its rightful place, she pulled on her coat, gloves and scarf, and they ventured outside. At lunchtime, Penny liked to walk Fischer before settling down to enjoy her lunch alongside a chapter of one of her current reads. Their afternoon walk varied depending on what village they were in that day, although their evening walk in Cherrytree Downs was always the same; across the village green, around the duckpond, and as far as the church and back.

Before they had ventured too far, Penny admitted defeat. The footpaths in Rowan Downs were untreated, with the result they were slippery to the point of being treacherous.

"Fischer, I don't know which one of us is going to fall over first, but I think it's likely to be me. I have never been able to do the splits and I don't want to learn now. Come on, back to the van we go."

From Rowan Downs, it was a three-mile drive to Chiddingborne, where Penny pulled up outside the Post Office just after two o' clock. She waved to the postmistress, who was moving two chairs onto the pavement, "Thanks, Mrs Dodds." The chairs served to reserve the library van a parking space, often to the annoyance of any other drivers hoping to park there in the hour or so before Penny arrived on a Monday. Woe betide anyone who tried to move the chairs, faced with the wrath of Mrs Dodds, those who tried, failed.

When Penny opened the doors the first couple of people filed inside, and Penny climbed out to talk to the others waiting in line, while Fischer remained in his seat barking a happy welcome to each patron. Some library members liked to browse themselves, but many relied on Penny for book recommendations. Based on their feedback about books they had read, Penny would make a selection for them or let them know when one was due back in.

"I've got a wonderful historical romance I think you'll love, Miss Farner," she said to one of her regulars. "A commoner plucked from obscurity to become Queen of England, whose sons were the lost princes in the Tower of London. How does that sound?"

Miss Farner clicked her dentures into place with her tongue. "Right up my street, Penny, thank you."

And so the book conversations continued, and when dusk fell around four o' clock Penny was quite surprised, the afternoon seemed to have flown by.

Penny and Fischer were alone in the van when a head peered around the door, 'Hello, Penny. Are you still open?"

She turned around and beamed, "Of course, Mr Kelly. We don't close until five. Come on in, it's nice to see you." She reached out her hand to help him up the steps. "What's it to be today, Mr Kelly? A stylish thriller with a stunning twist, or an intriguing mystery full of puzzling and sinister events?"

"Definitely the latter, Penny. Except it's not fiction I'm afraid. It's about Julia Wargraves. Have you heard what the coroner found?"

Penny raised a hand to her chest. Her heart was thumping so loudly she felt sure Mr Kelly could hear it. She had been so busy all afternoon she had not had time to think about the drama of Saturday night, or the plate of food and the bottle of cordial she had placed on a shelf in her locked garden shed. It was the only safe place she could think of to ensure an accidental tasting by either Fischer or Edward was avoided. As she could have predicted, Edward had dismissed her poison theory as a load of nonsense when she ran it past him the previous afternoon, but she hadn't wanted him eating the food just to prove a point.

"No, I haven't heard anything," she replied. "I wasn't sure how long these things take."

"Well it was obviously suspicious enough to go to the head of the queue. The preliminary autopsy report showed suspected cyanide poisoning, Penny. Julia Wargraves was murdered."

Penny gasped, "How did you find out, Mr Kelly?"

"Mrs Evans told me when I was at the bakery. She heard it from her daughter-in-law, who knows someone who works in the hospital. I saw you take the food and bottle of cordial from Julia's table on Saturday night. I guessed what you were up to. You and I have a similar taste in reading matter, remember?"

Penny nodded. The knowledge she had been right about Julia didn't give her any pleasure. To the contrary, its ramifications caused her to shudder. After an extended silence, she found her voice.

"I'll go to the police station straight away, after I go home and get the evidence. I'm sure Emma at the library will understand if I close a little early. Thanks, Mr Kelly, I really appreciate your coming to tell me. Do you need a lift home?"

He shook his head. "No, my daughter is parked just up

the street. Please let me know how you get on at the police station, and if there's anything I can do."

Penny was on the road out of Chiddingborne within minutes of Mr Kelly climbing down the library steps. She had called in to the Post Office to inform Mrs Dodds she had an urgent matter to attend to, but without giving any further details. Not that any were necessary, she knew word about Julia's death would spread through the downs like wildfire.

"I really want to get home then over to Winstoke as fast as possible, Fischer, but the weather is conspiring against us," she said as a flurry of snowflakes hit the windscreen, and Fischer gave a little whine as visibility reduced to six feet. "As if the roads weren't bad enough already. Well there's nothing we can do, we'll just have to take it steady and hope we don't have an accident."

When she eventually did land through the doors of Winstoke Police Station nearly three hours later, Penny was tired, hungry, and frustrated. The traffic in and out of the town had come to a virtual standstill due to broken down and abandoned vehicles. In the end, she parked in a supermarket car-park on the outskirts of town and walked the rest of the way with Fischer.

"Hello," she said, when she arrived at the desk. "I'd like to speak to someone regarding the death of Julia Wargraves."

Despite the fact she had lowered her voice, several heads in the waiting room turned her way. The desk sergeant recorded her details and nodded.

"Please, take a seat. Someone will be with you as soon as possible."

As soon as possible turned into forty minutes, by which time Fischer had started doing tricks to an amused audience of drunks and vagrants in the waiting room. Penny staved off her hunger with a chocolate bar and a cup of watery brown liquid, laughingly described as coffee, from the overpriced vending machines in the foyer. Just as she was considering calling Edward to bring her a survival pack from the stash he was stockpiling in his basement for Doomsday purposes, she was called into an interview room.

"I'm Detective Inspector Monroe. Thanks for coming in, Mrs Finch." The detective shook her hand and held out a seat.

"Miss," Penny found herself saying as she sat down. "It's Miss Finch."

"I apologise, Miss Finch. And who's this cute little fellow?"

Looking down at Fischer sitting in a perfect pose Penny smiled. The terrier now looked as though butter wouldn't melt, compared to his antics in the waiting room a few minutes earlier. Maybe he sensed Inspector Monroe was the top dog in this outfit, and a bit of decorum was needed. She got that impression herself.

"Fischer," she said. "He's my right-hand man. Say hi,

Fischer." The little dog lifted his right paw and barked once, then went to Penny for his good boy treat.

Inspector Monroe laughed, "What a clever dog. He's smarter than some of the criminals I've had to deal with. And talking of criminals, I believe you have information in connection with the death of Julia Wargraves? Please, start when you're ready and take your time."

Penny recounted the events of Saturday evening, from when she had rushed to Julia's side and detected the aroma of bitter almonds, to her taking the food and cordial from the table as possible evidence. Inspector Monroe listened intently throughout, jotting down notes.

"I've brought them in," Penny said, lifting the plastic bag she had used to carry the victuals, and passing it across the table. "Because, following my original fear Julia may have been the victim of foul play, I've since heard her death was indeed deliberate."

She studied Inspector Monroe's reaction, but his expression did not give anything away. "Thank you, Miss Finch. I appreciate your vigilance." He paused, and Penny thought he was about to say something else so leaned forward in anticipation, but he checked himself.

"I'll certainly arrange for these to be analysed and I'll be in touch to let you know the outcome. Oh, and Miss Finch?"

"Yes, Inspector?" For some reason, she felt her cheeks flush. Which was inexplicable considering the interview room was freezing cold.

"I'm new to the area and wondered if you could recommend anywhere for dinner?"

"Oh. Well there are several places in town, but I don't know them well enough to recommend them. However, if you want several cask ales to choose from, home cooked food in a traditional atmosphere, in the oldest pub in the South of England, then you can't beat The Pig and Fiddle in Cherrytree Downs," Penny replied.

"Good heavens, you don't work for the tourist board by any chance do you?"

Penny laughed, "No, I run the mobile library. But just a word of warning, you'll need a four-wheel drive to get there in this weather. It's only five miles but it's hilly and the roads are quite narrow in places, and the hedgerows high."

"No need to worry on that score. I like the way you think, Miss Finch. Back to the scene of the crime as it were. Yes, I think I shall patronise this pub of yours and see what's being said on the grapevine."

# FIVE

"How about this one, Mrs Potter?" Penny pulled out a book with an image of a man wearing a kilt on the cover. "It's set in the Scottish Highlands. There's danger, romance and time travel, and a woman who is torn between two very different men, one in each world. You won't be able to put it down. And if you like it, which I'm certain you will, there are plenty more books in the series. I can get them from Winstoke for you to read in order."

Mrs Potter squinted at the man on the cover. "Be still my beating heart. Is it raunchy?" Without waiting for Penny to reply, she whipped out her library card. "I'll take it," she said, waiting for Penny to remove the ticket and stamp the return date. "Otherwise, Edna Wilkins certainly will."

"Edna Wilkins certainly will what?" said a shrill voice from behind Mrs Potter, and the two women began to gently bicker.

Penny smiled. It was the same every week with these two elderly ladies, but it was well known they were quite good friends in private. She handed the book to Mrs Potter and filed the ticket she had removed from the book in the Borrowed folder for Hambleton Chase.

"Your turn, Mrs Wilkins," Penny said, her eye scanning the Harlequin section. She frowned as her mobile phone began to ring. Pulling it from her pocket, an unknown number flashed up on the screen. "Excuse me just one moment, Mrs Wilkins. I won't be long."

Stepping outside, Penny answered the call. Expecting it to be from a tele-marketer whose number she would subsequently block, she was therefore taken by surprise to hear Inspector Monroe's voice.

"Hello, Miss Finch? This is Inspector Monroe from Winstoke Police Station. We met yesterday evening, regarding Julia Wargraves?"

Penny took several steps away from the van. "Hello, Inspector. Yes, I remember." She was unlikely to forget the slow journey home from Winstoke the night before either. By the time she got back to her cottage, had eaten and seen to Fischer, it was past ten o' clock. She had only managed to read a few pages of her book before falling asleep with the bedside lamp on.

"I was wondering if you could come in to the station again today, Miss Finch? I'd like to speak to you in more detail about the events of Saturday night."

"I'm at work at the moment, Inspector, but I could call in later. Would about five-thirty be all right? I believe the roads around Winstoke have been cleared, so there shouldn't be any delays."

"Yes, that's fine, Miss Finch. I'll look forward to seeing you then."

"Okay, bye."

Hearing raised voices behind her, Penny turned around and made her way back inside the van to placate Mrs Wilkins. She might be a mobile librarian but the role meant she wore many hats, keeper of the peace being one of them.

"Thanks for coming in, Miss Finch. I appreciate your time." As well as his notebook, Inspector Monroe was carrying a thin buff-coloured folder. He sat opposite Penny in the same interview room as the night before, but this time the room was warm, courtesy of a small electric heater in the corner.

"No problem, I'm happy to help. And please, you may as well call me Penny. Everyone else does."

Inspector Monroe nodded, "Okay, Penny." He bent down and peered under the table. "And hello again, Fischer." He was rewarded with a happy bark and a thump of a tail.

Penny found herself wondering what the Inspector's first name was. She often thought some people's names suited them perfectly, and for others their name was at odds with their personality. Edward, her fiancé, definitely looked like an Edward. He hated it when anyone called him Ed and made sure to correct their mistake. Penny understood why.

Edward wasn't easygoing enough to be an Ed.

Inspector Monroe was speaking, and she jolted back to the present.

"The food and the bottle of cordial have been analysed, Penny, I put it to the top of the queue last night, and the results came back earlier. You were right, the cordial was laced with cyanide and a strong sedative, which is consistent with the coroner's findings. The food had not been contaminated, again evident by the fact that no one else at the party was taken ill."

Penny nodded, "I see."

"We're currently working on tracing the poison to the supply source," Inspector Monroe continued. "However, as cyanide is present in many common substances found around the home, that may not be straightforward. It's present in apple pips, just as an example, but the cordial was an apple and ginger presse from a local juicing company. It's unlikely to be the source, but all their stock is being recalled as a precaution."

Penny thought of the long queue for the cordials at the Christmas Market, and hoped Julia's death didn't end up putting the company out of business. "But you said Julia's cordial also contained sedatives, Inspector. Apple pips don't explain that."

"No they don't. It's possible she had put some kind of medication in her own drink and we're looking into that. However, the most likely explanation is that Julia was the target." Inspector Monroe gazed across at Penny, and she shifted in her seat. "Penny, are you aware of anyone who might have wanted to kill Julia, or did you notice anything unusual at the party?"

She shook her head. "I've been thinking about this a lot over the past few days, and I'm not sure I can add anything at this point. I wasn't sitting at Julia's table, but my friend Susie Hughes was. I only moved beside Susie when the dancing started and she was left alone at the table. A few people may have come and gone while we were sitting there talking, but we weren't paying attention." A sudden thought occurred her and her face fell. "Inspector, I hope you don't think Susie or myself are involved in this tragedy?"

She hoped she looked as indignant as she felt. Fischer let out a woof of support from under the table, and Penny could have hugged him.

Inspector Monroe regarded her with a bemused smile, and a dimple appeared in his chin. "I like to think after so many years on the force I'm a reasonably good judge of character. So at this point no, I don't think you're involved. We'll be speaking to your friend Susie and the other guests in due course." He paused. "You didn't answer the first part of my question, did Julia have any enemies you know of, any ongoing feuds that may have led someone to kill her? Middle-aged women in small communities don't get murdered without good reason."

Penny hesitated. Whilst she may have heard certain things

about Julia in passing, Penny paid little attention to hearsay and never engaged in gossip. "I think it's unfair of me to say anything that would tarnish Julia's reputation, Inspector, having had limited dealings with her myself. I always found her pleasant enough although there may be others in the surrounding villages whose words may not be so kind."

Inspector Monroe's pen hovered over is notebook, "Go on. What exactly do you mean?"

"I mean, I like to keep out of other people's business, Inspector. If you want to know the ins and outs of the Hampsworthy Downs grapevine, I'm not the right person to ask. On the other hand, I know some people who might be able to help. I can speak to them or give you their names, whichever you prefer."

Penny knew Susie had her finger on the pulse of the community goings-on, especially through her job at the newspaper. All the same, she didn't want to imply Susie had a loose tongue either.

"We'll be speaking to everyone concerned as part of our inquiries. Even so, any information you can provide would certainly be helpful, Penny. Look, forgive me if I'm being blunt, but you seem like an intelligent woman with your head screwed on properly. You had the nous to gather up critical evidence, for starters. So yes, if you could ask around and remain vigilant for any clues that might help with the investigation, I would be very grateful. Police resources in the area are limited, as you probably know."

Penny thought of bumbling PC Bolton in Cherrytree Downs and suppressed a smile. She couldn't imagine him being of much assistance to Inspector Monroe at all. Humphrey was good for putting up posters about missing pets, and dealing with schoolchildren pilfering sweets from the newsagent's, but that was where his talents stopped.

"In that case, I'll let you know if I hear anything," she said. She felt Fischer rub against her leg and could tell he was restless. "Will that be all?" she asked. "Fischer needs to visit the park."

"Yes, I think so." Inspector Monroe watched her get up. "Oh, and thanks for the dinner recommendation, by the way. The Pig and Fiddle's a good spot. Anywhere with a reading snug that serves good homemade cooking gets my vote every time."

"You're welcome," Penny said, pleasantly surprised that Inspector Monroe was a reader. "You should join the library if you like to read."

Inspector Monroe stood up and grinned, "I think I will. Come on, I'll see you out."

Outside, Penny phoned Susie while Fisher explored the park, stopping to sniff at every tree and bush, and jumping with great excitement into the great piles of snow that had been cleared from the paths. When she had updated her friend regarding the two visits to the police station, culminating in Inspector Monroe's request for help obtaining information about Julia, Susie sighed.

"It sounds very exciting, Penny, and right up your street, but honestly I'm up to my eyeballs right now. What with my job and the kids' homework, not to mention school plays and carol concerts, I'm not sure I'm going to be organised in time for Christmas never mind anything else. Playing sleuth, while appealing, just isn't possible as I don't have the time. Sorry."

"That's okay, don't worry. I thought that might be the case. I wanted to run something else past you anyway, about Christmas."

"Oh?"

"Would you and the children like to come for dinner at my parents' house with me and Fischer on Christmas Day?"

"Would I!" Susie replied. "You're a lifesaver, we'd love to! That's so kind of your parents, thank you so much. Please let me bring pudding though, it's the least I can do."

"Not necessary, but the more puddings the merrier as far as I'm concerned," Penny said. "Dad's a sucker for raspberry Pavlova, by the way."

"Deal. I've got to go, Penny, but I'll catch up with you soon. Will you be able to find someone else to help you out with the Julia investigation?"

"Actually yes. I think I know just the person. Mr Kelly has a lot of spare time on his hands, and he's got his ear to the ground in terms of the latest gossip. I'll give him a call. Bye, Suse."

"Bye, and keep me posted. Promise?"

"I promise." She hung up and called to Fischer, who came bounding over covered in snow. "Well, Mr Fischer Finch, you're about to become a dog detective. Let's see if you're as good at digging up clues as you are at clever tricks!"

"Woof!" Came the reply.

# Six

Coffee and cake at the Pot and Kettle cafe in Thistle Grange on Wednesdays was always a highlight of Penny's working week. After spending the morning in Holt's End and then travelling to Thistle Grange at lunchtime, it was her custom to make her way to Cobblers Lane after giving Fischer a good walk. There, those in the know could find the Pot and Kettle tucked between a doctor's surgery and a furniture upholsterer's, which inexplicably was more often than not closed. Fischer, meanwhile, was safely playing with his Thistle Grange chums, two rambunctious black Labrador puppies named Gatsby and Daisy. Their owner, Mr Sheridan, another literary buff, took Fischer for a few hours every Wednesday afternoon, rain, hail, snow or shine, to walk in the woods or play in his rambling garden, where Fischer chased rabbits, crows and anything else that moved. It was a perfect way for him to socialise with other dogs and he always came back tired but very happy.

That day, instead of cake, the waitress set a serving of roasted butternut squash and spinach quiche in front of Penny, with a side order of winter greens. When Penny had called Mr Kelly that morning to ask if he could meet her there, he had suggested lunch, and she had thought it a perfect idea. While her soup remained untouched in its Thermos in the library van, Penny knew it would be perfect as a light supper instead of cooking when she got home.

Mr Kelly gave an appreciative sigh as he tucked into his Shepherd's Pie, and Penny tasted her quiche, which had a spicy kick she wasn't expecting. She reached for her glass of water as Mr Kelly spoke.

"So what's the mysterious thing you wanted to talk to me about, Penny? I hope I'm not in trouble for the coffee stains on the last book I borrowed." Mr Kelly lowered his voice and leaned closer to Penny. "I had a minor tremor. Nothing serious I'm pleased to say, but I'm afraid the book bore the brunt of my shakiness."

Penny shook her head, "Not at all, Mr Kelly. Please, don't worry, those kinds of things happen all the time. I've seen far worse. You wouldn't believe the cookery books that come back splattered with cake mix. And the people responsible don't bat an eye."

"That's a relief," Mr Kelly said. "So, what's on your mind, Penny?"

Penny glanced around the room. Only a couple of other tables were occupied, and were both out of earshot by the window, but she lowered her voice all the same. "Remember you came to see me on Monday afternoon, about the coroner's report on Julia Wargraves?"

My Kelly nodded as he ate.

"The police have analysed the consumable items I gave them from the party." Penny's voice trailed to a whisper. "Julia's cordial was poisoned."

Mr Kelly spluttered and raised his napkin to his mouth. For a moment Penny was worried he was choking, and was poised to jump up and perform a Heimlich manoeuvre. She had only ever had to do it once before, when Dolly Murphy had choked on a boiled sweet in the van. Penny had managed to dislodge the offending item which had shot out like a bullet and hit a window. Dolly had recovered, which was the main thing, but a small crack in the glass remained as a permanent reminder of the incident.

Mr Kelly recovered himself before Penny had cause to act. "My goodness," he said, reaching for the teapot.

"Let me do that," Penny said, noticing his hand was trembling. She topped up his cup and watched while he added his own milk.

Mr Kelly took a sip. "This Julia Wargraves business has been playing on my mind. It's one thing to think someone might have been bumped off, and quite another finding out they actually have been. What a dreadful business. Do the police have anything else to go on?"

"I don't think so. Not at the moment, anyway." Penny filled him in on her visits to Winstoke Police Station and conversations with Inspector Monroe.

"Never heard of him," Mr Kelly said, cocking his head

to the side. "He's not from around these parts I take it?"

"No, he said he's new in town, but not where he came from," Penny said. "Up North somewhere, judging by his accent. The thing is, Mr Kelly, Inspector Monroe asked if I knew whether Julia had any enemies who might want her dead. Anyone she was feuding with, that sort of thing. I said I didn't, but I knew someone who might." She looked at him pointedly, hoping he would pick up the hint.

Mr Kelly chuckled. "You thought I might, did you? I do keep my ear to the ground, if I say so myself. There's not much else to do around here, apart from the daily crossword and reading. And walking of course, when the weather's better." He indicated over his shoulder to the window. "I can't go for my daily constitutional when it's like that outside, not unless I want another new hip."

He pushed his plate away, and leaned across the table closer to Penny, eyes twinkling as he continued. "What I'm trying to say is, I'd love to help the police in any way I can. What do you have in mind?"

Penny swallowed her last bite of quiche and set her cutlery together. She smiled, "That's great news, Mr Kelly, I really appreciate it. You have more time on your hands than I do, so I suppose it's a question of putting our heads together and seeing what we come up with. We can't be too obvious, mind you, in case we tip the murderer off."

"Good point," Mr Kelly said with a nod. A few seconds later, his expression faltered. "The problem is, Julia was one of those women who got people's backs up whatever she did and wherever she went. Not that that means they were all lining up to kill her, of course." He rubbed his chin. "For instance, how about the time Mrs Montague bashed into Julia's car, and Julia reported her for careless driving? Oh, and when Julia started rumours that old Harry Barnes was a flasher. He wasn't of course he just wore that old mac all the time, but Harry's son was furious. He went over to Julia's place and loud words were spoken. It was all Mrs Duke next door could talk about for days. Then there was poor Mrs Sykes trying to live on a meager pension by purchasing her clothes second-hand. Of course Julia criticised everything she wore and made her feel quite grubby and ashamed. As far as Julie was concerned, if it wasn't brand new, with the correct label then it wasn't worth bothering about. It was a shameful thing to do."

"Gosh, I had no idea," Penny said, surprised to learn about these petty episodes. Although the rumour about Harry Barnes could have had terrible repercussions if Julia had been taken seriously. "It seems I'm more out of the loop than I thought. I can't imagine Mrs Montague killing anyone, all the same. I don't think she would give two hoots what anyone accused her of. She once told me she had driven an aid vehicle all the way across Europe to Sarajevo and back in the Nineties. Careless driving is about the least likely thing she would be guilty of."

"True, and the police never took it any further. What I mean is, I'm sure there are plenty more examples of Julia's belligerence. And on the face of it, almost anyone from Hampsworthy Downs could have been responsible for her death. Most folks were at the party, and it wouldn't have been hard to slip something into Julia's drink. There were so many people coming and going, a little splash of something in her bottle while she was up at the buffet..." Mr Kelly shrugged. "Finding the killer isn't going to be easy. I suspect Inspector Monroe knows that, which is why he is enlisting eyes and ears on the ground, so to speak."

Penny paused while the waitress cleared the table. "That was delicious, thank you," she said, smiling up at her.

"Would you like anything else?" the waitress asked them.

Penny eyed the glass counter in the corner before turning back with a sigh. "Much as I would like my usual slice of coffee cake, I think I'm going to have to pass. I'll fall asleep at work this afternoon if I eat anything more. How about you, Mr Kelly?"

Mr Kelly raised a hand. "I couldn't eat another bite. My compliments to the cook."

When the waitress had gone, Penny pondered what Mr Kelly had said about the difficulties the police faced in finding Julia's killer. "Inspector Monroe did say the police will be interviewing people who were at the party," she said. "But I definitely got the impression he thought an insight into local goings-on might help give the police a better perspective on the case. Although..." she hesitated to voice aloud the niggling thought she couldn't get out of her head.

"Go on," Mr Kelly said, with an encouraging smile. "If we're going to make any progress, you'll have to share what's on your mind, my dear."

"You know what they say," Penny began. "It's always..."

"The spouse? Exactly what I was thinking myself. I taught Stanley Wargraves when I was an assistant teacher, you know. He was a clever boy, but full of self-importance, even then. His astuteness seems to have stood him in good stead as a businessman though. I believe his Estate Agency has the local property market sewn up. But I find it difficult to imagine him as a killer."

Penny did a quick mental calculation as to Mr Kelly's age. Stanley Wargraves was in his fifties, and Mr Kelly had been retired for several years, so she put him at no older than seventy.

A slow smile spread across Mr Kelly's face, which creased the tiny lines at the corner of his eyes. "I'm sixty-eight," he said, reading her mind. "I retired a couple of years early, thanks to my dodgy hip. But since the replacement, I feel a lot younger. And in here," he said, tapping the side of his head with his forefinger, "I'm still twenty-five."

"Aren't we all, Mr Kelly. I'm thirty-nine but certainly don't feel it, and my parents are more advanced in years than you and they say exactly the same thing."

"Age is just a number, Penny. What makes life worth living is friends and family and helping others. Now, what do you plan to do next?"

"I was thinking of going to visit Stanley Wargraves tonight to pay my respects. The Wargraves' house isn't far from where I live. The reason I was wondering about whether Stanley might have a motive is that his secretary was all over him in the hall after Julia died. Maybe it's my imagination, but it struck me as being overly-familiar behaviour for work colleagues. Unless of course, there's something else going on between the two of them." She looked around again to make sure no one was listening. "Forgive me, if you think I've spoken out of turn."

Mr Kelly let out a laugh, "My dear, I think no such thing. That's what I mean about the importance of saying whatever is on your mind. There's a time and a place for keeping your opinions to yourself, and this isn't one of them. Going to visit Stanley sounds like an excellent starting point, in my opinion."

Penny heaved a sigh of relief. She knew Mr Kelly was probably right, but gossip didn't come naturally, her instinct being to keep her opinions to herself.

"I, on the other hand, have no qualms about speaking out of turn," Mr Kelly announced. "I think I'll ruffle a few feathers and see where it gets me. It won't be hard to plant the seeds of a conversation about Julia with several people I suspect weren't fans of hers. It should be interesting to see what comes out of it."

"Perfect, but do be careful, there's a murderer loose," she said. "I'll look forward to hearing what you come up with. And I'll report back on Stanley, of course. I'm so pleased you agreed to help me, Mr Kelly. Thank you. I think we'll make a great team."

"Indeed, we will." Mr Kelly grinned back at her. "Whoever killed Julia Wargraves better watch out, eh?" He motioned to the waitress. "You'd better get back to work, Penny. I'll take care of the bill."

"No, I insist, Mr Kelly. Please, let me," Penny stood up.

Mr Kelly waved her away, "Certainly not. You get the next one. I haven't had quite so much fun in ages. You've given me a new purpose, Penny, the least I can do is pay for lunch."

# SEVEN

"Now then Fischer, we're going somewhere different for our walk tonight," Penny announced as she attached his lead. "I know you like tearing across the green to tease the ducks, but you'll have to be on your best behaviour this evening. We're heading somewhere quite fancy and naughty dogs are not allowed."

Fischer hung his head and Penny immediately felt a pang of guilt. "Oh, Fischer, I'm only teasing you know. You are the best dog ever!" She crouched down and scooped him up in hug. "I know you're a good boy, but Stanley Wargraves doesn't, and we don't want to upset him. He has a big garden like the one you were playing in today, but his isn't for running around in or chasing things. It's a show garden, and that means..." Penny wondered what it did mean, and then it came to her. She sighed, "It's just for show, Fischer, not for playing in, as ridiculous as that sounds. But we both need to be on our best behaviour as we have to ask some awkward questions."

There was also the fact that Stanley might be a murderer and Penny didn't want Fischer in his bad books, but she decided not to voice that concern aloud, in case it tempted fate. Not to mention the fact Fischer seemed to understand her every word. It was uncanny how human her little dog was.

A slight rise in temperature that day had seen the start of a thaw, and Penny and Fischer made their way on foot to Stanley Wargraves' home without mishap. When they reached the green, they turned towards the shops instead of their usual route which would have taken them past the Christmas tree, but even so, Penny could see the snowman had been decapitated.

When they arrived at Stanley's pretty cottage, the lights were on and several cars were already parked outside. The Wargraves had lived in one of the large detached cottages in the most expensive part of the village for as long as Penny could remember, although their home was the only one in its row of five that had a modern one-storey extension at the back. Penny remembered the outcry it had caused when Stanley had applied for planning permission several years before, and all of the neighbours had objected. Even so, the plans had been rubber-stamped by the Planning Committee at Hantchester Borough Council in record time, and a large glass combined kitchen and living area, with bi-fold doors opening onto the garden, appeared several months later. Julia had ignored the jibes about Stanley having friends in high places through his business connections, and extolled the virtues of 'bringing the outside in' to anyone who would listen. Apparently she had also extended an invitation to the editor of House and Country magazine to feature the cottage in a future issue. So far the invitation had been ignored.

"You'll have to stay in the porch, little man," Penny said in a low voice to Fischer when she rang the doorbell. "I won't be very long, okay?" Fischer stared back up at her for a brief moment before turning his head away. Anywhere Penny usually took him he was allowed inside, so Penny knew that in Fischer's eyes, it meant they weren't with friends. And for Fischer, that was no fun at all.

The door was opened by Ruth Lacey, who regarded Penny with a puzzled expression, but recovered herself quickly. "Penny, how nice to see you. Do come in, but remove your boots first, we don't want to ruin the floor," she said, stepping aside. "It's mostly people from work here, but Stanley will be so touched you came. Follow me, and I'll see if I can find him for you."

Ruth led Penny down the hallway past the door to the vast kitchen, where she could see a table laid out with tea and baked goods including a magnificent Christmas cake, and into a formal sitting room. Several people stood in huddles, talking in muted tones. Stanley was standing by the fireplace, above which, a huge framed portrait of Julia looking down over the proceedings caused Penny to catch her breath.

"It's very lifelike, isn't it?" Ruth said, noting Penny's reaction. "Julia always liked to be the centre of attention." She leaned towards Penny and whispered, "Between you and me, it gives me the creeps. I'm going back into the kitchen."

Penny approached Stanley, who turned to her without a trace of a smile. He looked better than the last time she had seen him but still not himself. "Penny. How kind of you to come."

She held out her hand and shook his offered one, "Stanley, I'm very sorry for your loss. I can't imagine what you're going through, but if there's anything at all I can do, please ask." Looking up into his sad eyes, she wondered if he was capable of killing his wife and the grief was all an act. If so, it was a good one. Then she remembered Stanley was a founding member of the Amateur Dramatics Society, and in every production played an excellent leading role. She dropped his hand.

"Stanley, is there somewhere we can talk in private?"

If Stanley was confused, he didn't show it, and instead simply nodded. "Of course. My study is next door." He wandered into the hallway and led Penny through a door opposite the kitchen, from where Penny caught Ruth craning her neck in an attempt to see what they were doing.

The study door clicked shut, and Stanley motioned to a couple of leather armchairs. "Please, take a seat, Penny."

Penny settled herself on the creaking leather, and Stanley sat opposite her, sighing heavily as he sank into the chair. His eyes were bloodshot, and Penny could smell alcohol on his breath.

"I'm glad you came, because I wanted to thank you," Stanley said. "Inspector Monroe told me you had the foresight to remove some items from the hall when you were leaving after… well, you know. What made you think of it?"

Penny shrugged, "I'm an avid mystery reader, it goes with the job, and I recognised the smell of almonds for what it really was."

They sat in silence for a few moments, Stanley waiting for Penny to say something more, and Penny wondering how to broach the subject of Julia's enemies. She thought of how Mr Kelly had urged her to speak her mind, and she took a deep breath with the intention of doing so when Stanley suddenly blurted out, "This is all my fault. If I'd paid Julia more attention, maybe she wouldn't have acted the way she did, rubbing people up the wrong way. I took care of the business, built it up from scratch you know, but it took up a lot of my time. I realise now I probably neglected my wife even though that wasn't my intention. I just wanted to provide for her, give her nice things."

His eyes were beseeching Penny for some kind of reassurance, or was it absolution? Either way, Penny couldn't give it to him. Looking around the study with its walnut desk and panelled walls, and from what she had seen of the kitchen and the sitting room, she was certain of one thing; everything was top of the range and the best that money could buy. But there was no getting away from the fact it was all purely material wealth. For all its surface gloss and sparkle it was obvious to Penny there was a lack of real love and affection here.

"Stanley, there's no doubt you provided for Julia very well. No expense has been spared in your home, and I'm sure she enjoyed your annual cruises. And of course she adored being able to shop in London whenever she wanted. Half the village population would be waiting when she returned to see what had caught her eye."

"It was usually shoes. She adored the ones with the red soles," Stanley said, staring at a spot somewhere behind Penny's head. "Despite the price tag, I liked them too, because they made her happy." He caught Penny's eye before his gaze trailed down to her rainbow striped socks, "What size feet do you have, Penny? Ruth's a six, so they won't fit her. Julia was a five, you see."

"They won't fit me either," Penny lied.

Stanley looked around the room as though seeing it for the first time, "Julia did everything in the house you know. I wouldn't even know where to begin. Ruth's been helping out of course, but how I'm going to manage now I just don't know."

"It's early days," Penny said, her tone gentle. "You don't have to think about all of that now, Stanley. Just take it one day at a time. It's lucky you've got Ruth to help."

There must have been something, although completely unintentional, in Penny's tone because suddenly Stanley sat up with a jolt, "What's that supposed to mean?" His eyes narrowed, "I hope you're not implying anything, Penny, because if that's what people are saying, I'll..."

Penny waited, but Stanley didn't finish. Instead he shrank back into the seat, raking a hand through his thinning hair, "Forgive me, Penny, I've hardly slept since this happened. Things are just getting on top of me and I'm not coping very well. I didn't mean to be so short with you."

"It's my fault, I wasn't clear," Penny said, leaning forward. "I just meant it's nice you have so much support from your work colleagues. You need support and assistance at a time like this. But, if you don't mind me saying so, I don't think drinking is the answer. It's a depressive and will only make you feel worse in the long run."

Stanley stared at her in disbelief, before his face crumpled, "You're right. About the booze, I mean. But it's the only thing that numbs the pain. As for my so-called work colleagues, they're paid employees, Penny. Which means they'll do whatever I ask them. It's why they're here now, making tea and smalltalk and bringing me whiskey every half hour. It's nothing more than being nice to the boss. Ruth's the only one of the lot of them who's genuine. I'm sure the others talk about me behind my back. Not that I really care. I mean what's the point of any of it now Julia's gone?"

Stanley's voice broke and Penny sat back and waited

while he wept into his handkerchief. She felt terrible being witness to his raw grief, but she still hadn't asked the questions she'd come to ask.

Eventually Stanley pulled himself together and Penny took a deep breath. If she didn't ask the question now she never would.

"Stanley, I don't mean to be insensitive, but I need to ask you a question. Inspector Monroe inquired if anyone had a grudge against Julia and I'm afraid I couldn't answer. Do you know?"

"Quite a few I suspect," Stanley replied sadly, giving his eyes a final wipe and replacing his glasses. "Julia tried to keep it from me but I heard the gossip too. She wanted me to believe she was popular and well liked, but she went about it the wrong way and I could never find the right way to tell her. She thought she needed to impress people you see? Have the best or be the best at everything to win friends, but it had the opposite effect. That's why she entered so many competitions. She was victorious in practically everything she entered, but it caused petty rivalries and outright jealousy and she ended up garnering enemies alongside her trophies."

Penny was beginning to realise that minding her own business, and not reading the thrice-weekly Hampsworthy Gazette from cover to cover, weren't exactly assets when it came to detective work. She was clueless about Julia's other noteworthy achievements.

"I knew she won the Best Kept Garden, and rightfully so your garden is stunning, but what other competitions did she win?"

"Her roses always won first prize in the flower show, and the last two years her leeks and marrows have won the home-grown produce section. She's won the Sugar Hill Treasure Hunt three times, the only times she entered incidentally. And then there's the Cherrytree Downs Christmas Cake Competition, although someone else will get a chance to win this year. Julia only finished decorating her entry last week. I checked if she could win posthumously if I entered it, but Major Colton ruled it out. It's terribly unfair, if you ask me, but those are the rules. Apparently, Mrs Templeton kicked up too much of a fuss."

"Mrs Templeton?" The name rang a bell with Penny, but she couldn't place her.

"Yes, she was a dinner lady at Winstoke High School before she retired. Lives in one of the original workers' cottages beside the Montague place."

"Oh yes, I know who you mean now," Penny said, picturing the tall woman with fierce red hair and a temper to match. "She worked at the High School when I was there. She made an excellent sponge cake topped with jam and coconut, if I remember rightly. It was delicious with custard."

"That's the one. She's been runner-up in the Christmas

Cake Competition for the last five years. Maybe she finally sees her chance for glory."

Penny was about to ask Stanley more about Mrs Templeton, when Ruth put her head around the door.

"Stanley, people are asking for you," Ruth said. "What should I tell them?"

"Tell them I'll be right there." Stanley stood up and straightened his sports jacket. "Penny, please excuse me. I hope we can catch up again." He reached out and shook her hand, "I really do appreciate your visit."

Penny watched them leave, Ruth ushering Stanley out while whispering something in his ear. *Nice to the boss my foot*, Penny thought. As for Mrs Templeton, she sounded like she warranted further investigation. She needed to speak with Mr Kelly.

# EIGHT

Penny's attempts to elicit information about Julia Wargraves from one of the weekly Cherrytree Downs library regulars the following day, evoked an unexpected reaction that made her rethink her approach.

"Julia Wargraves loved that book," she murmured to Maureen Bates, a renowned gossip and font of local knowledge, who was perusing the Chick Lit shelf. Maureen had pulled out a paperback with an illustration of a woman in towering heels laden with shopping bags on the cover, and was reading the blurb on the back.

"Julia once told me she thought that series of books about a woman's adventures in shopping and life mirrored her own," Penny went on doggedly. "I'll never be able to look at any of them again without thinking about her."

Maureen shoved the book back onto the shelf and glared at Penny. "You've just put me off reading it. Honestly, Penny, it's bad enough everyone talking about that dreadful woman without you starting too. If she were alive, she'd love the attention she's been getting this past week. Now she's spoiled my Thursday visit to the library as well. That's after me thinking I saw her ghost earlier, I almost fainted in the street I was so shocked!" Maureen began to take a series of short, sharp breaths. "Look what you've gone and done you silly girl. You'll have to send for my Harold to come and get me."

Penny quickly unfolded one of the two camping chairs she kept in the van for the older patrons, "Please sit down, Mrs Bates, I'm so sorry I upset you. Let me fetch you some water. It must have been a terrible experience, thinking you saw Julia like that. It's so hard to come to terms with such a tragic event in a small community like ours. I shouldn't have said anything. Please, forgive me."

Maureen scowled at her and shook her head, "Don't look at me like that. I'm not losing my marbles just yet. If you saw someone dressed head to toe in Julia's clothes you'd get a fright too. That leopard coat of hers is unmistakable. Luckily, I realised it was Mrs Sykes. Looking quite pleased with herself I might add. Julia's things are quite a step up from the usual charity shop standard, I suppose."

Penny poured some water into a plastic cup and handed it to Maureen, who took a sip.

"Stanley's sent Julia's clothes to the charity shop already? That seems fast," Penny said, voicing her thoughts aloud. "Julia's not even buried yet."

Maureen shrugged. "I might take a look in myself, if Mrs Sykes hasn't already snagged the lot. Julia did have some nice knits, although they're probably hand wash only and who has the time for that?" She stood up and handed Penny the empty cup. "I'll be off. I'm feeling better, although no thanks to you. My day has been ruined. And I'd have a few things to say about Julia Wargraves, except I'm not one for gossip and I won't speak ill of the dead."

Penny helped her down the steps. "Are you sure you don't want someone to get your husband to come and meet you?" Harold Bates was never hard to find, he arrived in the Pig and Fiddle at opening time and stayed there most of the day, nursing a pint of real ale. Whether it was to escape his wife's tongue, no one knew for sure.

"Never mind him," Maureen said, scurrying away towards the green. "Fat lot of use he is."

Penny sat in the chair recently vacated by Maureen Bates and Fischer jumped onto her knee for a cuddle. He'd made himself scarce as soon as the woman's voice had become angry. "Well Fischer, that didn't exactly go according to plan. I don't think I'll mention Julia again if that's the sort of response I get. It all seems so much easier in the mystery books. Maybe it's better to just listen and learn."

"I hope you had more luck with your inquiries about Julia than I did, Mr Kelly," Penny said to him the following day. "Although, I did have an interesting conversation with Stanley."

It was her day off, and they were back in the Pot and Kettle, this time with Fischer curled up asleep under the table. The cafe owner was a dog lover and adored Penny's little dog, who was always so well-behaved.

Penny found herself indulging her tea and cake habit while Mr Kelly stuck to just the tea. "I don't have a sweet tooth," he had explained to her, almost apologetically when the waitress took their order. "But you tuck in."

She didn't need to be told twice, and ate with relish while Mr Kelly recounted what he had uncovered during the previous couple of days.

"It wasn't hard to get people talking about Julia," he began. "Since her murder is already the main topic of conversation, and I do get about, you know. I'm in Cherrytree Downs every morning at the bakery, and one or more of the other villages later in the day. My daughter likes to joke she's my personal taxi driver, but really I just catch a lift here and there when she's on her health visitor rounds."

Penny recalled Mr Kelly's daughter, Laura, having been in a minor road traffic accident a couple of years previously, when her car had skidded on an icy road. Although Mr Kelly didn't mention it, Penny suspected he was worried about Laura driving in the current wintry conditions. It wouldn't surprise her at all if some of the journeys Mr Kelly took with his daughter were mere excuses to make sure she was safe, rather than out of any necessity on his behalf. Widowed for many years, his devotion to Laura and her young family was evident.

Mr Kelly took a small notebook from the inside pocket of his jacket and opened it, scanning several pages of neat cursive text. "I wrote everything down," he said, peering at Penny over the top of his glasses. "Not that my memory's bad, at least not to my knowledge. But it's easier to keep a track of everything, and the police might want see it."

Penny spoke up, "That's a good idea. I think I should do that too. Go on." She added hot water to her infusion of apple and cinnamon tea and took another bite of her lemon poppy seed cake.

"There were a few snide comments, as expected," Mr Kelly said. "One of the highlights being her use of a Blue Badge to park in spots reserved for the disabled. That got a few backs up, let me tell you."

"I can imagine. Although I suspect she's not the only one guilty of that. I've always thought there are a lot of Blue Badges in this neck of the woods. Sometimes it seems as though every other car has one."

Mr Kelly raised an eyebrow, "Well, not every disability is obvious of course, but in Julia's case I'm fairly sure she didn't need one. No one knows how she got the badge, but Mr O'Connor who's in a wheelchair, was berated by a mother for parking in a Parent and Child space when the disabled spots at the supermarket were full. Apparently Julia had parked her fancy SUV over the line and taken up two spaces."

"That was inconsiderate," Penny said. "What else?"

"Just a few grumbles, nothing too serious. Her competitive spirit didn't go down very well with some of the gardening community, the rest of whom are generous when it comes to helping each other out." He chuckled, "Local legend has it Julia bought up all the local manure supply one year, just so nobody else could get their hands on it. She used it on her roses and her prize-winning vegetables. It caused quite a stink; pun intended."

Penny smiled, "But none of that would be a motive for murder, surely?"

Mr Kelly shook his head. "I shouldn't think so. What was more interesting was my conversation with Mrs Evans at the bakery. You know they live in the next house along from the Wargraves'?"

"Yes," Penny nodded. "I'll tell you about my visit to see Stanley in a moment. You go on."

"Mrs Evans was… how shall I put this…" Mr Kelly lowered his voice. "Let's just say there was a lot of the old nudge, nudge, wink, wink innuendo regarding a dolly bird who visited Stanley at the house several times while Julia was away recently, looking after her sick mother."

Penny almost choked on her cake, "Dolly bird? I'm not sure if you can say that these days, Mr Kelly." She wiped her mouth with a napkin. The moniker was in keeping with Mr Kelly's generation, but she suspected it would still probably offend plenty of people.

"Never mind all that politically correct nonsense, a lot of it's being taken too far in my opinion. Anyway, you know what I mean." The sides of Mr Kelly's mouth turned up and his eyes twinkled with playful mirth.

"I think I do. Did you get a description of the... woman by any chance?"

"Indeed, I did. I thought you would never ask." He read from his notes. "Blonde, voluptuous, in her early thirties, drives a..."

Penny couldn't resist interrupting, "Red Mercedes sports car, by any chance?"

Mr Kelly grinned, "How did you guess? But on a more serious note, you know, I know, and Mrs Evans knows, the woman she was describing was Ruth Lacey, although she had the tact to pretend she didn't. There's something else. Mrs Duke, the Wargraves' neighbour on the other side, told me she had heard Stanley and Julia arguing of late. It seems they weren't getting along."

"Where did you see Mrs Duke?" Penny asked. "Did you call into her house?"

"Not exactly. I walked past a couple of times, until I spotted her twitching the curtains and then I waved. She came out and we had a quick chat. Of course, Mrs Duke was another one who had issues with Julia in the past, what with the cat episode, but I have to say, I think Julia would be a trying neighbour regardless." Mr Kelly snapped his notebook shut and returned it to his inside jacket pocket.

"I'm confused," said Penny. "what was the cat episode?"

"Julia accused Mrs Duke of encouraging her cat do its

mess in her garden. There was a bit of a ruckus as Julia liked her garden to be kept pristine for the Best Kept Garden Award, which as you know she's won for more years than I can count. But in the end the feud between the two women blew over when the cat died."

Penny sighed, "The more I hear about Julia, the more contrary she sounds. For what it's worth, I always found her perfectly pleasant, although a little stand-offish. She brought her library books back on time, and even had a nice word for Fischer occasionally."

"I know what you mean. All of her braggadocio never bothered me either, it struck me she was trying to make up for the shortcomings in her life." Mr Kelly gave Penny a sad smile. "We all have our own truths. It seems to me that Julia irked some people by preying on their weaknesses to make herself feel better, and she knew exactly which buttons to press to get the desired result. Of course, what upsets one person is water off someone else's back. But I'm intrigued. Just what was worth so much to someone that Julia had to die for it?"

Immediately, Ruth Lacey sprang to Penny's mind. Was Julia's husband worth killing for?

She filled Mr Kelly in on her visit to see Stanley and what she considered as Ruth's territorial behaviour. "Another thing," she added as an afterthought, remembering what Maureen Bates had told her about seeing Mrs Sykes dressed in Julia's clothes. "What if it wasn't Stanley who gave Julia's things to the charity shop? What if it was Ruth, wanting to clear out all memories of Julia as soon as possible?" Penny could feel her heartbeat quicken, certain Ruth's motives regarding Stanley Wargraves were not at all innocent.

Mr Kelly patted her arm, "Let's not jump to conclusions, Penny. We can easily find out by asking at the charity shop. For all we know, Julia herself may have taken some of her things in before she died. And don't forget that Ruth, as Stanley's secretary, had a legitimate reason to be visiting Stanley at home, even if Julia did happen to be away at the time."

"What about the raised voices Mrs Duke heard?" Penny reminded him. "You have to admit, it sounds suspicious."

"I'd settle for circumstantial at present."

When she thought it over, Penny had to concede Mr Kelly was right, for the moment at least. "Oh, I almost forgot," she said, wishing she'd had Mr Kelly's foresight to start an investigation notebook. "I need to tell you about Mrs Templeton, Julia's rival in the Christmas Cake Competition, and then we can decide what to do next."

# Nine

"Thanks for coming to the Christmas Cake Competition with me," Penny said to a gloomy-looking Edward. She had banked up the wood burner and adjusted the damper, so it would still be glowing when they returned. She was cooking Edward dinner later, a medley of roasted vegetables with lemon and coriander couscous, then perhaps a drink before he went home. She had a bottle of white wine chilling in the fridge.

Edward wrapped his scarf around his neck twice, tucked the ends inside the corduroy collar of his navy quilted jacket, and eyed the wood burner, "I'd prefer to be warming my feet by the fire on a cold Saturday afternoon than eating cake with little old ladies," he said, smoothing his hair and putting on his tweed cap. "I just hope no one's poisoned this time."

Edward's reluctance to walk across to the Village Hall with Penny was more than offset by Fischer's exuberance. Her four-legged companion knew they were going somewhere as soon as she picked up her keys. He proceeded to dash to the front door then back to Penny, trailing his lead and running rings around her feet. "Fischer, you're going to trip me up," she laughed, looking around for her handbag. "Now sit there like a good boy a moment while I find my bag."

Penny found her bag in the living room and tucked her new notebook and pen inside. Edward, who had followed her, gave her a poignant look. "Taking it a bit seriously aren't you? Your unofficial, unpaid, murder investigation duties, I mean." He pulled on a pair of gloves. "Mind you, I suppose John Monroe needs all the help he can get. I can't believe he has the position he has, considering he failed to finish university."

Penny had been surprised when Edward had mentioned he knew Inspector Monroe from their university days in Manchester. But it also settled her curiosity about his first name. She thought John suited Inspector Monroe perfectly, he struck her as a solid, reliable, trustworthy and straightforward sort of man.

She sighed, "Just because he dropped out of university, doesn't mean Inspector Monroe is lacking in intelligence, Edward. I'm sure he didn't achieve his rank without a lot of skill and hard work. Third-level education isn't the only path to success you know, and snobbery about qualifications is really a thing of the past. The largest social network on the planet was founded by a college drop-out, and the word documents and excel spreadsheets you use for work every day were created by another. They did all right for themselves didn't they?"

Edward acknowledged her argument with a dismissive grunt which just riled her even more.

"Next, I suppose you'll tell me my degree was wasted, now that I'm driving a mobile library van around the countryside?" She placed her hands on her hips, taking in Edward's bewildered gaze.

"I just think you could do a lot better career-wise, that's all," he said, with a frown. "But I do admire your allegiance to your causes, Penny. I just don't think the rewards are worth all the hard work you put in." He shrugged apologetically. "This murder business for example. Agreeing to help the police is all well and good, but what's in it for you?"

Penny softened a little at Edward's genuine confusion. It was just like him to be baffled by something that didn't have a monetary value or personal benefit attached to it. Trying to explain to him that doing something she believed in, for no reason other than good citizenship and wanting to do the right thing, was pointless. It would also take too long, and the Christmas cake competition would be over if they delayed any longer.

"I just want The Downs to be a safe place to live," she said finally, walking over and kissing his cheek. "I'm lucky I've got you to protect me, but some of the older residents have no one. They should be able to sleep safely in their beds at night, don't you think?"

"Well, when you put it like that… " Edward said, returning her kiss with one planted firmly on her forehead.

"Come on then, let's go and do our good deed for the day. The sooner we meet this Mrs Templeton, the sooner I can get back and watch the television."

The mood in the Village Hall was sombre, not surprising considering most of the attendees had been present the previous weekend when Julia had died. But to make matters worse, someone in their wisdom had erected the Winner's Podium right on the spot where she had collapsed.

The podium itself consisted of upside-down crates covered with red tablecloths, where the winner and runner-up would stand to have their photos taken for the Hampsworthy Gazette, and Penny was pleased when she spotted Susie walking around chatting to some of the entrants. Although Susie's official title at the paper was Editorial Assistant, they both knew it really meant glorified general dogs body, so Penny was thrilled to realise some of the quotes her friend would gather on her rounds, would most likely make their way into the final copy. Even though she would receive no official credit.

She gave Susie a wave before making her way to the first of the two long tables where the cakes were displayed. The festive decorations adorning the hall from the ill-fated dinner remained, although with the lights on they looked old and tired, rather like some of the ladies standing behind their entries.

"What are we supposed to do?" Edward whispered to Penny as they approached the first cake in the line-up. "They all look the same to me."

Surveying the line of white-iced cakes laid out on trestles covered in green tablecloths, Penny suppressed a grin. For once, she and Edward were in total agreement, the only thing distinguishing one cake from the next were the decorations on top, varying in levels of gaudiness. Penny's personal taste was for minimal adornment and to let the taste do the talking, but she supposed that didn't make for a very striking competition entry. The cake toppers on display ranged from entire nativity scenes to snowmen, angels and Christmas trees, plus the time-honoured Father Christmas, with a wild-card unicorn thrown in for good measure.

"Just smile and say they look lovely," she said out of the side of her mouth. "And when we get to Mrs Templeton, leave it to me."

Edward dutifully complied and had several cake owners fawning over him by the time they were half way down the first table. His tall, good looks, combined with his eloquent compliments pertaining to presentation and cake-making dedication, charmed every competitor over the age of sixty.

"You're laying it on a bit thick," Penny pointed out, after Mrs Sykes was the second person to ask if Edward was a new judge that year. "If Major Colton thinks you're trying to muscle in on the judging, he might take umbrage."

"Penny, it's a village cake competition not the Nobel Peace Prize."

"Yes I know, but he takes it very seriously."

"Well if he gets punchy you can set Fischer on him."

Penny looked down at the little dog sitting by her foot, the epitome of a perfectly trained and lovable puppy, and laughed, "Well I suppose he could smother him with kisses if we need him to."

"I think we're here, Penny," Edward whispered.

Penny turned and smiled at the woman standing behind a majestic two-tier cake, decorated with a holly and ivy wreath made from green hand-cut leaves and red berries, with a shiny red ribbon wrapped around the side. "Mrs Templeton," she said, wide-eyed. "This is my favourite cake so far. You must be in with a good chance of taking home the top prize. Has Major Colton been around yet?"

Mrs Templeton beamed with pride, "He's been around the hall once, Penny, but he doesn't do the final judging until the end when all the members of the public have had a chance to take a proper look. Then we cut him a little piece to taste. The taste is just as important as how well the cake is decorated."

"Yes, of course," Penny said.

She looked up at Edward, who gave Mrs Templeton a sage nod. "Absolutely," he added, for effect. "If you don't win this year, Mrs Templeton, I'd say you've been robbed."

Penny nudged Edward to be quiet, but it was too late,

Mrs Templeton had instantly taken a shine to him and leaned across the table to share his confidence. "Wouldn't be the first time, dear. You could say I'm used to it."

"Really?" Edward moved closer and lowered his voice to a conspiratorial whisper. "Why's that, Mrs Templeton?"

"You obviously never saw Julia Wargraves' baking," Mrs Templeton sneered. "Her cakes weren't a patch on mine but she had an unfair advantage, so she did."

"Golly," Edward gulped dramatically and it took Penny a herculean effort not to roll her eyes. "That's dreadful. Did you report it to the judge?"

"It's the judge who was the problem," Mrs Templeton hissed. She gave a withering look up the table at the line of ladies standing behind their cakes. "Why do you think these old bats are fluttering their eyelashes at every man who comes along? Because that's what Major Colton likes, that's why."

Edward folded his arms, looking grave, "And you think that's why Julia always won, Mrs Templeton, because she was flirting with Major Colton?"

"Mm hmm." Mrs Templeton pursed her lips, "And the rest."

"Well, good luck this afternoon, Mrs Templeton," Penny interrupted, grabbing Edward firmly by the elbow. "Although I'm sure you won't need it. If your cake tastes as good as it looks it will be very hard to beat."

"Thank you, Penny." Mrs Templeton turned to someone else who was admiring her creation, and Penny and Edward worked their way down the rest of the table. When they got to the end, Edward sighed, "I can't face another table full of cakes and niceties, Penny."

"That's okay, I don't think I can either," Penny said, steering him toward the edge of the hall where there was less chance they'd be overheard. "You were great with Mrs Templeton, and personally I think her cake deserves to win, it's first class. I can certainly understand why she'd be annoyed if she produced that standard every year with nothing to show for it." She paused for a moment, spotting Susie a few feet away. "Although, so far we've only her word for it about Julia's inferior baking skills. There was a Christmas cake laid out at Stanley's the other night when I was there. It looked pretty impressive to me, although I didn't taste it."

Edward motioned towards the buffet table at the top of the room. "I'm going to go and have a cup of tea and a mince pie or three. I may as well get my entrance fee's worth. Between you and me, I feel a bit sorry for these women. All that effort, and if Major Colton's as bad as Mrs Templeton says, then it's all for nothing unless they provide him with a certain level of personal attention. That was the inference I took, at least."

"You and me both. Maybe you would be a better judge than him after all," she teased. "Something to think about for next year?"

Edward shook his head and muttered something inaudible as he walked off.

"Hi, got a minute?" Susie appeared at Penny's side and launched into an update on her latest divorce woes. Penny kept one ear on Susie and one eye on Major Colton who was doing his final judging round, until a voice came over the PA system.

"Ladies and Gentlemen, your attention please. Major Colton will now announce the winner of this year's Christmas Cake Competition."

All eyes turned to the podium, where Major Colton, dressed in tweeds, looked every inch the quintessential English country gent. He tapped the microphone a couple of times before speaking, and the sound reverberated around the draughty room.

"Hello everyone. It's been a sad week for The Downs, and one none of us will forget in a hurry. Let us all take a moment to reflect in silence on the memory of Julia Wargraves, a valued member of our community and past Christmas Cake Champion extraordinaire."

Heads were bowed, but Penny's eyes were on Mrs Templeton, who she noted stared straight ahead, face expressionless.

After the silence Major Colton continued with his speech. "Thank you, as always, to everyone who entered this year's event and all of you who have come out on this freezing afternoon to support them. Funds raised are going to a great cause, the Hambleton Chase summer fair. It's been a lot of fun, and not a soggy bottom in sight." There were a few groans in the audience, but Major Colton continued, undeterred. "And now, the moment you've all been waiting for. The standard was superb this year and it was very close, but this year's runner-up is someone you're all used to seeing up here on the podium. A big hand, please, for Mrs Templeton!"

Any murmurs were drowned out by polite applause, and Mrs Templeton, wearing a face like thunder, came forward to accept her trophy whisk and take her place on the lower of the two crates.

Major Colton's joviality continued as he announced the winner. "It's a new face on the podium, but a familiar one in Hambleton Chase. A huge Hampsworthy Downs thumbs up to... Mrs Potter!"

Penny turned to Susie, "That's a surprise, isn't it? Was her cake any good? Edward and I didn't make it that far."

Susie shook her head, "It was average at best. I'm not sure what Major Colton's up to, but his judging methods have upset a few people. Poor Mrs Templeton looks like she's about to burst into tears."

A woman on the other side of Penny spoke up, "At least Julia Wargraves was a decent baker, regardless of what was going on between her and Major Colton. But Mrs Potter's cake was a joke. The Major's moved on all right and mighty quickly, that's all I can say."

"Hello, Mrs Wilkins," Penny said. "Do you mean the Major and Julia were, um, involved?"

Mrs Wilkins raised an eyebrow, "There was some sort of carry on, if you ask me, for her to win five years in a row. Julia wasn't as squeaky clean as she made out, but only the Major could tell you for sure. Now if you'll excuse me, Penny, I'm going to leave, before Mrs Potter comes over to crow."

"I have to go as well," Susie said, planting a kiss on Penny's cheek. "James is dropping Ellen and Billy back at home at four o' clock and I want to speak to him in person, instead of through a lawyer for a change. I'll catch up with you next week, and you can tell me how your investigation's going. Bye for now."

Penny reached for her notebook. The investigation was becoming more and more interesting by the day.

# TEN

"Mark and Ruth Lacey are joining us at the Pig and Fiddle for lunch," Edward announced on Sunday, stamping the slush from his boots onto the mat at Penny's door. "Are you ready to go?"

"Fischer is, I'll just be a moment," Penny said, standing aside to let Edward in. She gathered up her things, congratulating herself on letting Edward think it had been his idea to invite Mark and Ruth to join them in the pub. All it had taken was a couple of casual remarks from her the previous evening and Edward had sent Mark a text message. She idly wondered if a similar tactic would work for their infrequent date nights? it would be nice to go somewhere other than the Winstoke Cinema. Perhaps the new Bistro in Thistle Grange.

"What's this?" Edward said, picking up the open journal from the coffee table. Penny had invested in a second notebook, one in which she could scribble down her thoughts regarding the murder investigation in an attempt to pull together the mounting information. The first would still be used for the legitimate interviews. "You're writing a diary?

Aren't you a little old for that nonsense?"

Penny swiped the notebook out of his grasp and snapped it shut. "If I were, it would be none of your business," she said, opening her bag and cramming it in amongst the packets of tissues, pens, mints, two random library books and the box of Earl Grey teabags she carried around at all times. It rarely happened, but she liked knowing she was never far away from a decent cup of tea.

"All right, calm down," Edward mumbled, tapping the piece of tissue paper on his chin where he had nicked himself shaving. He shaved daily, even on weekends and holidays, as part of a meticulous grooming routine which had recently expanded to teeth whitening.

On that subject, Susie had already expressed her thoughts to Penny several weeks before. "Is Edward having a mid-life crisis?"

Penny hadn't been sure what she was getting at, "No, why?"

Susie had rolled her eyes, "If he doesn't stop soon, his teeth will glow in the dark. You should tell him, Penny, teeth like that belong firmly in the realms of twenty-something reality television contestants, not forty-something accountants."

"They're his teeth," Penny had pointed out. "If it were me, I wouldn't let him tell me what to do with my appearance. I think I owe him the courtesy not to try and change him either."

But Susie wasn't about to let it drop, "Didn't you say he mentioned several times to you about going to the slimming club with me? Or joining the gym at the Winstoke Leisure Centre?"

"That's exactly what I mean," Penny had said. "And I told him I'm healthy, and quite happy with my shape. If he wants somebody he can change, he can find another partner."

"Good for you," Susie had commented. "If James said that to me, I'd have had another piece of cake and told him where to go. Not that it matters now." And then she had burst into tears.

Suddenly Fischer let out a frustrated howl, pulling her back to the present. "Yes, we're going now," she grinned, bending down to ruffle his fur. "To the Pig and Fiddle, your favourite place. Where else do you get fussed over and get to be the centre of attention every time we visit?"

"Just about everywhere he goes," Edward said, watching them with a half-smile. "I think I'd like to be Fischer sometimes. Ready now?"

Penny reached out and pulled the tissue paper off Edward's chin. "Yes," she said, nudging him towards the door. "Let's go."

A roaring fire in the stone fireplace welcomed Penny, Edward and Fischer as they entered the Pig and Fiddle, and several other Sunday lunch regulars nodded in greeting when they entered. Harold Bates was sitting at the bar as usual, and the Evans family had a table by one of the steamed-up windows in the conservatory. Edward had to duck to stop his head hitting the exposed timber beams on their way into the dining room, where Mark and Ruth Lacey were already seated. Fischer, meanwhile, skipped across the uneven stone floor, his route to their table hampered by regulars calling him over to pet him or feed him a scrap of their lunch after he'd done one of his tricks.

Mark Lacey stood to shake Edward's hand when they approached, and he kissed Penny warmly on the cheek. Ruth, looking up from her menu, gave them both an awkward smile. "Hi," she said in a quiet voice. "Good to see you both." She took a sip of her white wine, averting her gaze to the menu she was holding in her other hand.

"Ruth's not been feeling very well," Mark said, by way of apology for what Penny considered to be, if not rudeness, then a definite lack of warmth from his wife. "It's been stressful for her, having to pander to Stanley Wargraves' demands all week. On top of her normal workload, Stanley seems to have put her in charge of the funeral arrangements, as well as expecting her to entertain and cater for the never-ending stream of people calling at his house every evening."

"That's a bit of a cheek, don't you think, Penny?" Edward made his indignation known with a frown and a stern gaze around the table.

"Absolutely," Penny murmured. She didn't know Ruth

well, but the subdued person sitting opposite her was a far cry from the assertive woman who had been fawning over Stanley when she'd visited several nights earlier.

"It's not a big deal, Mark," Ruth said, throwing him a venomous stare which did not go unnoticed by Penny, although Edward, busy trying to attract the waiter's attention, missed it. "Stanley's in no state to manage anything right now. I don't mind helping out in a crisis. After all, I'm the only person he can rely on."

Mark rolled his eyes and turned his attention to Penny. "While Ruth's been looking after Stanley, I've been living on microwave dinners all week." He patted his portly stomach, "I'm wasting away to nothing as you can see. It's the full roast for me, I think. What takes your fancy?"

Penny checked the list of handwritten Daily Specials attached by paper-clip to the regular menu. Mrs Barnes, the cook, catered well for vegetarians and there were always several choices on offer. The Pig and Fiddle was popular with tourists as well as locals, however it looked like the weather had kept people away. While the temperature had hovered above freezing for several days, the forecast was for a bitterly cold front to return, with another dump of snow to follow. Several tables were still available in the dining room, usually full by that time on a Sunday afternoon.

"I think I'll have the roasted vegetable quiche," Penny said, setting her menu down. The pints of ale Edward had ordered for himself and Mark had been served, along with a bottle of wine for the table, and he poured Penny a glass. Polite small talk ensued after a waitress had taken their order, with Fischer proving to be a welcome distraction when the conversation faltered, due to him rubbing ankles under the table.

"I hope that's Fischer playing footsie with me, and not you, Penny," Mark grinned. "I don't think Edward would be too pleased about that."

"No danger of Penny playing footsie," Edward said, before taking a sip of his pint. "Isn't that right, Penny?"

"Definitely not," Penny confirmed. "I mean why have a dog and bark yourself?"

Mark laughed, "Touché, Penny."

Eventually the men's conversation turned to football, which left Penny and Ruth nursing their wine in awkward silence.

"Hello, Penny," a familiar voice suddenly said, and a man stopped at the end of their table. "I thought you must be around somewhere, when I recognised Fischer doing his tricks over by the bar. Unless he comes to the pub by himself, that is."

Penny looked up at the rugged face of Inspector Monroe, unshaven and smiling. The flickering flames of the firelight were reflected in his dark eyes and she found herself catching her breath before she was able to reply. "He doesn't, I mean, not as far as I know," she said, wondering when Fischer had escaped from under the table, why she was suddenly unable to form a coherent sentence, and what it was about Inspector Monroe that made the heat rise in her cheeks. Four sets of eyes rested on her, making her feel even more self-conscious. "I believe you already know Edward, and this is Mark and Ruth Lacey," she said, collecting herself. Turning to the Lacey's, she smiled, "This is Detective Inspector Monroe. He's investigating the murder of Julia Wargraves."

Inspector Monroe tactfully ignored the sound of Ruth spluttering on her wine, and shook hands with Edward, Mark, and then Ruth once she had recovered. "Nice to meet you," he said, with a nod. "Enjoy your lunch."

Edward spoke up, "Won't you join us, John? The more the merrier."

"No, I won't interrupt, but thanks for the invitation," he said, his eyes lingering on Penny just a moment longer than necessary.

"So how is Stanley bearing up?" Penny asked Ruth, when Edward and Mark's conversation turned to golf, and Fischer was once more settled at her feet. "I'm sure he appreciates all the support you've been giving him, even if he hasn't had a chance to thank you properly. When the dust settles, he'll realise everything you've done for him."

Ruth's eyes narrowed, and when she spoke her voice was slurred. The bottle of wine on the table was almost empty, although Penny was still on her first glass. "You'd think so, wouldn't you?" Ruth said, with a vacant gaze. "I'm not so sure though. I thought I knew him, but grief brings out a strange side of people. He's taken Julia's death much worse than I expected. The way he used to talk about her sometimes you'd have thought he'd be glad to see the back of her."

Mark lifted the wine bottle and topped up Ruth's glass with the last of the wine, patting her shoulder, "Don't go getting all maudlin, sweetheart. And I'd take what anyone says about their spouse with a pinch of salt. Look at us for instance. Just because we don't shout it from the rooftops, doesn't mean we don't have a good marriage."

"Uh-huh," Ruth said, before taking a large gulp of wine.

"Great, here's the food," Penny said, glad of the diversion. Her quiche looked delicious and was served with a crisp salad, although she declined a second helping of sweet potato fries in order to leave enough room for dessert. The Pig and Fiddle's Sticky Toffee Pudding was exceptional, and she never passed it up.

Ruth was quiet during the meal, and Mark gave her several worried glances, offsetting her silence with humorous stories about his job as a surveyor with Hantchester Borough Council. His easygoing manner and way with words had Penny in fits of laughter on several occasions, and with an enthusiastic audience he milked the gaffes of his colleagues for all they were worth. She decided she liked Mark Lacey a lot. His wife, she wasn't so sure about.

When they had finished eating and Fischer was snoring gently under the table, Edward curled an arm around her shoulder and she leaned against him, happy to relax in the pub's ambient surroundings for a while longer. They were in no hurry to get home, and the only cooking she did on Sunday nights was her pot of soup for the week ahead, which was already gently cooking.

All of a sudden Ruth got up abruptly, and shoving back her chair rushed away from the table with her hand covering her mouth.

Mark gave them an apologetic smile, "She can't hold her wine," he said, looking around for the waitress. "Do you mind if we get the bill? Sorry about this, I'm going to have to take her home."

"I'll just go and see if Ruth's alright," Penny said, after Mark and Edward had split the bill on an itemised basis, worked out by Edward using the calculator on his phone. "She's been gone for ages."

"Thanks, Penny," Mark said as she got up. She heard Mark say something to Edward as she walked away about her being a smashing girl, but didn't catch Edward's response.

In the Ladies room there were only two cubicles, one of which was vacant, but the sound of muffled sobs could be heard from the other. "Ruth?" Penny said softly. "Are you okay in there?"

The sobbing quietened, followed by the toilet being flushed. "Go away," Ruth said. "I'm fine."

"Mark's worried about you. What do you want me to tell him?"

The lock on the toilet door clicked, and a sullen looking Ruth emerged from the cubicle. Her eye makeup smudged and her face blotchy from crying. "Look at the state of me," she said, glancing in the mirror before rubbing her eyes. "I look like I've been dragged through a hedge backwards."

"That's always a good look in this part of the world," Penny said. "In fact some blow-ins strive to perfect it."

Despite herself, Ruth smiled, "Sorry," she said. "My behaviour this afternoon has been terrible. I'm not usually such a lush. It's just..." Her face crumpled once more.

"Don't worry," Penny said. "Like Mark said, you've been under a lot of pressure lately. Do you want to talk about it?"

"It's not what Mark thinks," Ruth said, sniffing. "Honestly, if you knew the way Julia used to treat Stanley you'd understand what I mean. She had him running around in circles trying to keep her happy, but nothing he did could please her. He worked night and day to make money faster than she could spend it, and she still made a fool out of him."

Penny washed her hands at the basin and took her time drying them with the paper towel, "What do you mean, she made a fool out of him? Did Julia do something to embarrass him?"

"If you really want to know, you'd be better off speaking to Major Colton," Ruth said quietly, running the tap and picking up the soap. "And whoever else she was running around with on those trips of hers. Is it any wonder everyone at work has closed ranks on Stanley this week, when we're the ones who witnessed first-hand what she put him through? Heard him begging her not to leave him, when any man with a shred of dignity would have divorced her long ago?" She looked back up at Penny and shrugged. "It's amazing what some people will put up with. He said if she wasn't around things would be different. But he's got what he wanted so why isn't he happy?"

It was a question Penny couldn't stop thinking about for the rest of the day.

# ELEVEN

Two things struck Penny while she was waiting for Mr Kelly at the tee-pee inspired pop-up cafe in Chiddingborne Christmas Market the following afternoon. First, Christmas was five days away and she still had several gifts to buy. And second, how devastated Mark Lacey would be when his wife was arrested for Julia's murder.

Penny had spent much of the evening before sifting through the clues as they pertained to Ruth, pondering how she could have obtained the poison, then telephoning Mr Kelly to discuss the matter, but she had not considered the fallout of such an arrest on her husband. It was clear to her, from spending time at the Pig and Fiddle with them, that Mark was oblivious to his wife's feelings for her employer. Feelings, which Penny suspected were either not reciprocated by Stanley, or not as strong as Ruth had imagined before she had done away with Julia.

The tent buzzed with shoppers peeling off their winter layers in favour of the heat from the elevated log pit in the centre of the space, around which were scattered wooden tables and benches adorned with vibrant red poinsettia. The music coming through the sound system was piped throughout the market, vintage Christmas tunes that reminded Penny of her own childhood. The excitement of hanging up her stocking by the fire on Christmas Eve and leaving out a mince pie and a glass of milk for Father Christmas, as well as a carrot for Rudolph. Plus the empty pillowcase left at the bottom of her bed, which would be miraculously filled in the morning, would be forever etched in her memory. She knew her biological clock was against her, but if she was honest with herself she didn't really mind, it was enough to enjoy the atmosphere and observe other's children tearing the wrapping off their gifts from Santa's Grotto, with flushed cheeks and infectious laughter, and their absolute belief in this magical man.

"Sorry I'm late, Penny," she heard a muffled-sounding Mr Kelly say, and looked up to see a figure wrapped in a dark wool coat, hat, scarf and gloves. He set several shopping bags onto the table before removing his hat and scarf, at which point his smiling face came into view. "It's been a very busy morning. One which I'm looking forward to sharing with you." His gloves and coat were next to go, and he arranged his things on the bench. "But first things first. Shall we eat?"

"Absolutely," Penny said. "I've been saving myself all morning. I still consider lunches out quite a treat, even though I seem to have had quite a few of them recently. Believe me, that's not the norm. Fischer's beside himself with all the attention he's been getting." She nodded to Fischer a couple of feet away still attached to his lead, where he was entertaining a couple of toddlers strapped into their buggies beside the table where their mothers were having lunch. Rubbing his nose against the children's feet, he set one of them off into giggles before starting on the other. In return, he was happy to eat whatever food they discarded as a result of their merriment, clumsiness, or both. Since they dropped more of their mini-hot-dogs than went into their mouths, Fischer was on a winning streak.

"Tis the season," Mr Kelly said, looking up at the blackboard where the menu was written with chalk pen in a fancy hand. "I like to drag it out as long as I can."

"I'm afraid it's crept up on me a little this year," Penny confessed, after making her selection. She decided on the Mushroom Wellington, while Mr Kelly chose Seafood Chowder with wheaten bread. "I'm usually more organised, but I've been preoccupied with the... you know." A waitress wearing a Christmas jumper and a reindeer antler headband had appeared to take their order, and Penny tapped her notebook to indicate what she meant.

When the waitress had gone, Mr Kelly leaned in, "I do know, and I was glad you called me last night to give me an update about Ruth and Mark Lacey. I have more time on my hands than you, so was happy to take the trip to see Inspector Monroe this morning, like you suggested. I got an update from him as well as filling him in on your suspicions about Ruth. He did say that Ruth's reaction when you introduced him yesterday hadn't escaped him."

Penny's eyes lit up. She was certain she was on the right track, especially if Inspector Monroe had noticed Ruth's strange behaviour too. "Were the police able to trace the poison?" She knew that would be a big part of the investigation. If the source of the poison was found, it could lead them straight to the murderer.

Mr Kelly shook his head, "That's not going to be straightforward I'm afraid. The police spoke to the local pharmacist who said cyanide salts can't be bought over the counter, but cyanide is present in many common household and garden chemicals and pesticides. As for the sedative that was mixed in with it, it's available on prescription to any number of the local population." His brow furrowed. "Which doesn't narrow it down at all."

"That does leave the net wide open." Penny was disappointed, but not surprised. "It sounds as though anyone can simply make a deadly concoction from products in their cleaning cupboard and pills in their bedside drawer." Then an idea suddenly occurred to her, "I wonder if there's a way we could get into Ruth's house and check her bathroom cabinet?"

Mr Kelly paused while their food was served. He buttered his wheaten bread, waiting for the steaming bowl of chowder to cool. Penny, after calling Fischer to return and settling him under the table with a chew, tried her Mushroom Wellington. She knew it was an easy dish to prepare and resolved to make more of an effort to vary the range of vegetarian dishes she cooked for herself at home. Cooking for one was an excuse not to go to the effort of being very adventurous with her cuisine.

"Well, let's not do any breaking and entering just yet," Mr Kelly said with a smile, after dipping his spoon in his chowder and adding enough salt and pepper to make it to his liking. "All we've really got is pure supposition and conjecture and a few educated guesses, which may or may not prove to be correct."

"Yes, you're right. I suppose if we moved around the clues enough we could make them fit anybody."

"Precisely, but we aren't doing this alone, in fact we are just here to help the police not the other way around. Inspector Monroe seems to be on the ball. Nice chap, too."

Penny nodded, "I agree. I noticed when I was walking through the market on my way in, that the stall selling Julia's cordial is open again. I take it that means there was no contamination in the source products."

"That's right, but they had to check as a precaution. If the cordial had been tainted a lot more people would have been affected. The other thing Inspector Monroe said was that the poisoned bottle of cordial you brought in was covered in fingerprints." Mr Kelly paused and took a sip of water before continuing. "But there's no way of knowing if

Ruth's were present without fingerprinting her. As she's never been arrested for any other crime, her fingerprints are not on file. The same goes for everyone else in the villages nearby. The police can't go fingerprinting everyone in Hampsworthy Downs, there'd be a revolt and cries of invasion of privacy."

"What about Mrs Templeton?" Penny asked.

"He agreed she may have had a motive, but she wasn't at the party." Mr Kelly flicked through his notebook and stopped at the most recent page. He scanned the text using his finger, before tapping it half-way down. "Here we are. The police have gone through the entire list of ticket sales and spoken to someone from every table, and will be speaking to the rest in due course. There were some no-shows, like your Edward for example. Mrs Templeton usually attends with some of the dinner ladies she used to work with, but one of their group confirmed she was never intending to go to the dinner this year. Her son had tickets for the pantomime in Winstoke. When Julia was killed, Mrs Templeton was in the dress circle of Winstoke Palladium with him and his family. Inspector Monroe has ruled her out as a person of interest."

Penny turned to her own notes, perusing her scribbles. "Stop me at any point, Mr Kelly, but this is what I'm thinking. Ruth's behaviour makes me suspicious she has a thing for Stanley, which may or may not have turned into an affair between the two of them. On that basis her motive would have been to get rid of Julia in order to have Stanley for herself. She told me Julia treated Stanley badly, and insinuated she was cheating on him with Major Colton, and possibly others. That ties in with what Mrs Wilkins told me at the Christmas cake competition. It also makes the Major someone we should probably speak to, do you agree?"

"Absolutely." They had both finished eating, and Mr Kelly moved their plates to the end of the table. "I should be able to help with that. Major Colton's wife was my cousin, and when she was alive my wife and I saw them often. Although we've lost touch in recent years." He gave Penny a tight smile. "My social life's not as lively as it used to be since I became a widower, although it sounds like the Major can't say the same. It's just one of those things, couples and singles tend to congregate separately whatever age group they fall into. Let me call the Major and ask if he'll see us. I don't expect it to be a problem."

Penny hesitated, "But what if Major Colton was Julia's lover and murdered her in a crime of passion? He might not be so keen if that's the case."

Mr Kelly chuckled, "Indeed. We can't rule it out but knowing the Major I can't imagine it somehow. He was always very laid back in matters of the heart, much to my cousin Christine's chagrin. I'm not sure why she put up with him to be honest, but I suspect him being away a lot suited them both. It seems to me, any crime of passion was more likely to have been committed by Julia's husband rather than the Major. Especially if Stanley was being cuckolded and was jealous, or just plain angry about it."

"Good point. Or, maybe Ruth and Stanley were in on it together and Stanley got cold feet?" The more Penny thought about it the more confused she was. Mr Kelly, on the other hand, was his usual imperturbable self.

"The truth will out," was all he said, pulling an old fashioned phone from his pocket. "Are you available tonight if the Major is free? It's probably best if we keep things moving along. Time is of the essence with a murderer on the loose."

Penny thought for a moment, "I'm supposed to be meeting Edward, but I'm sure he'll understand."

As she watched Mr Kelly punch a telephone number into his phone, which had no smart features whatsoever, Penny tried to think of any phone numbers she knew by heart. Apart from her parents, who had had the same number since the telephone was first installed, there were none, and she found herself impressed with Mr Kelly's memory. Sometimes the old fashioned ways were the best as she realised how lazy people had become with the advent of the digital age.

When Mr Kelly began to speak into the handset, Penny fastened Fischer's lead around a table leg and wandered over to the counter. She picked out several miniature chocolate logs to take home and paid the bill.

Mr Kelly was on his feet pulling on his coat when she returned to the table. "The Major can see us this evening," he said. "Do you mind picking me up on the way?"

"Not at all," Penny said. "Pike's Cross at seven o' clock?" The crossroads in Rowan Downs was a well-known landmark. According to local folklore, it was where the highwaymen of bygone years waited to pounce on their prey. It also marked the road to Pike's Farm, one of the largest in the area, and which had been passed down through many generations of the same family. She calculated if she stayed on in Chiddingborne after work, she could come back to the market and finish her gift shopping and still make it to Rowan Downs in plenty of time.

"Perfect. Thanks for lunch, Penny. I'll see you later. Goodbye, Fischer."

# TWELVE

Rowan Downs, three miles from Chiddingborne en route to Cherrytree Downs, was more of a hamlet than a village. Its population, one-hundred and thirty-eight at the last census, lived in a smattering of houses around Pike's Cross, its centre, where communal facilities were limited to a post box and a bench with a plaque commemorating Rory Pike, 1930-2006. Teenage residents, not that there were many of them, congregated on the bench in the evenings weather permitting, older folks using it while waiting for the twice-daily bus service in either direction. Locals liked the fact Rowan Downs was a blink-and-you'll-miss-it sort of a place, meaning most traffic was pass-through and not many cars stopped there during the busy tourist season in Spring and Summer.

It was for that reason various commercial plans had been vetoed over the years, its innate charm was in its simplicity. The trip to the shops in either Cherrytree Downs or Chiddingborne was worth it for the inhabitants who did not want their tiny community becoming a stop-off point for day trippers, and who were happy to point people in the direction of the other villages, as the nearest places to park their cars and spend their money.

The beauty of Rowan Downs was not lost on Penny, but she preferred the convenience of being able to walk to the bakery, the newsagent's and the pub, all easily accessible from her cottage. Living on Hampsworthy Downs was part of her fibre, and its rich variety of characters coloured-in her world. She had enjoyed being away at university in the late nineties, but loved returning for the holidays when she had her first taste of working in Winstoke Library as a summer job.

A fixed-term contract opportunity after graduation with the university library as an assistant held no sway for her, even if her romance with Robert Parker had not failed in their final year. When she later heard he had become a hotshot broker in the City, specialising in trading futures and options, she knew she'd had a narrow escape. It was a line of work she had always considered a clever smokescreen for gambling with other people's money.

"Move over, Fischer," she said, bringing the van to a stop at Pike's Cross. Mr Kelly had spotted their approach and was standing by the side of the road with his thumb stuck out. She leaned across Fischer and opened the door, "Hop in, Mr Kelly." She waited for him to clamber up and secure his seatbelt, and smiled as Fischer jumped onto his knee, turned in several circles then settled down.

"That takes me back a few years," she said, pulling back

onto the road. "Don't tell my parents, but I may have hitched a lift or two in my time, especially when my student grant was running low. I'm not recommending it these days, except to say you're safe with me. I have no prior convictions."

"Thank goodness for that." Mr Kelly stroked Fischer, who lay resting his head on his lap, something he only did with people he was very comfortable with. Edward's attempts at bonding with Fischer, and there had been quite a few in the months since the little dog had come into Penny's life, usually ended with Fischer wriggling out of his grasp. "It's this one," Mr Kelly said, pointing to an unmarked lane not far beyond Pike's Cross. "Past the cottages and keep going until you get to the stone house at the end."

The lane had borne the full brunt of that afternoon's snowfall, which had drifted in places to produce walls of shimmering white, and Penny was glad of the van's winter tyres. She had only had to use snow chains once in all the years since converting the trusty VW into the library van, when a twenty-first-century Ice Age had descended on the Downs for a couple of months. Schools had been closed and many isolated homes were cut off, and Penny had ended up bringing emergency supplies to some outposts as well as a weekly dose of reading. It was times like that the library service was so much more than Books on Wheels. It had been a lifeline for vulnerable locals.

She had never had reason to be down the lane where the Major lived, and the first sight of his home was all the more impressive for it. A traditional red-brick build with half a dozen towering chimneys soaring skyward, Mr Kelly informed her it was at least two hundred and fifty years old in its present incarnation, but the core was a medieval timber frame, and the whole thing was Grade II listed. It had been in the Major's family for generations.

The now bare tendrils of creepers were visible on the brick surrounding the entrance and Penny imagined how impressive the sight would be when everything was in full bloom. Snow-topped lumps and bumps in the adjoining garden suggested manicured grounds with walls and hedgerow features, and the house emitted a welcoming glow, the leaded windows illuminated by lamps on the inside, and the twinkling lights of a Christmas tree.

By the time they had climbed out of the van, the Major had flung open the front door and was waiting for them on the top step, drink in hand.

"George, old chap, good to see you," the Major said to Mr Kelly, slapping his back. Greeting Penny with a handshake, the Major's face beamed. "Penny, what a delight. Welcome to Thornehurst Grange. Or as I like to call it, home. I'm sure we've met on occasion, but please forgive me for not remembering the details. I'm not much of a reader, so that can't be it, but my memory's a fright. Come in out of the cold and bring this wonderful little dog inside with you." He peered down at Fischer, who was pawing at his trouser legs, and Fischer scampered inside eager to explore this new space.

The house was warm and unimposing considering its age and plethora of dark oak beams, the disarray lending an air of eccentricity rather than messiness. Random objects appeared to have been set down and forgotten about; a pair of spectacles resting on the carved newel post, a single upside down boot in the umbrella stand, and a half-eaten sandwich on the stone mantel in the cosy sitting room where the Major bade them sit and make themselves comfortable. A tray with a teapot and china cups and saucers was set out on a side table, and there was even a chewy dog toy lying on the rug which Fischer pounced upon.

"I took the liberty of making tea," the Major said, indicating the tray. "Although, I was hoping you might care to join me in something stronger." He held up his glass by way of confirmation. "George, can I tempt you with an eggnog or a hot toddy? How about you, Penny?"

"Tea's perfect for me, thanks," Penny said. She was glad to see there were no biscuits or cakes on offer, with the amount of lunches she had been taking recently, she'd look like the side of a barn by the time the case was closed. She'd already given the miniature chocolate logs she'd bought earlier to Susie.

"Not eggnog," Mr Kelly said, squinting at some family photographs dotted around the room. "Make mine a brandy. Just to keep you company, you understand."

"Excellent. Be right back." The Major strode across the room before abruptly coming to a halt and turning around again. "Sorry, Penny, I forgot to bring in the Christmas Cake. I have rather a lot of it after the competition on Saturday. You wouldn't believe how generous the contestants are. I've got enough to see me through to next Christmas." He let out a hearty laugh that was hard not to smile along with.

Penny's attempts to refuse cake were useless, and when the Major returned, she resigned herself to devouring what was probably the finest Christmas cake she had ever tasted.

"This is delicious, Major," Penny said as she took a bite of the expertly crafted wreath she had so admired at the competition.

"Ah, yes, the winning entry. Clever woman that Mrs Potter."

Penny glanced at Mr Kelly in surprise, and he shook his head slightly to warn her not to say anything. He was probably right, it would only add insult to injury for poor Mrs Templeton to know the Major, with his frightful memory, had mixed up the entries. And really, when all was said and done, a village baking competition was insignificant compared to a murder inquiry.

The Major relaxed in a wingback chair once they were all settled with refreshments. He had even produced a dog treat for Fischer, who wolfed it down so quickly it barely touched the sides, and was now snuggled on the rug near the Major's feet chewing the dog toy.

"Now then, do tell me. To what do I owe the honour of this visit?" His raised one leg and placed his foot across his other knee, displaying tartan socks. "I haven't had such a mysterious phone call since Lady Brightwell asked to see my roses."

Mr Kelly looked surprised. "Really, Hugh? I didn't know you were a gardener."

"They were Christine's roses," the Major admitted, his expression faltering. He glanced at a framed photograph on the table beside him, where he was standing with his arm around his wife at a family event. "They became a bit of an obsession for me, after she passed. I couldn't save her from the dreadful disease ravaging her body, but by golly I could do my best by the roses." He raised an eyebrow at Penny. "I hope you never have to experience losing a loved one, my dear, but sometimes it's the small things that keep you going through the dark days. George knows what I mean."

Mr Kelly nodded in silence, and bowed his head a moment, blinking repeatedly. Penny felt a tightness in her chest as sadness pervaded the room. Eventually Mr Kelly gathered himself, and clearing his throat spoke up.

"We wanted to talk to you about Julia Wargraves, Hugh. Penny and I have been helping the police with their inquiries. The local grapevine tells us you and Julia were more than just friends."

Penny watched the Major's reaction. He sighed and gazed away for a moment, before addressing Mr Kelly and Penny with the faint traces of a smile. "Lovely woman, Julia. Were we friends? Yes. Good friends? Probably. I met her through gardening, funnily enough. Spotted her wandering around the garden centre one day, like a lost soul, and we got talking. It went from there, really."

"Care to elaborate, Hugh?"

Penny admired Mr Kelly's directness and was grateful for the family connection.

"We all have our troubles, George. You and I know better than most how life can turn just like that," he snapped his fingers to demonstrate, and Fischer looked up. "I envy you, did I ever tell you that?"

Mr Kelly shook his head.

"You were a good husband, George, your conscience is clear. I can't say the same for myself. It was only when Christine was gone I realised what I'd lost. I've been living with the guilt ever since."

"We all do our best, Hugh." Mr Kelly said, looking at the Major. "But what's that got to do with Julia?"

"I wanted to help her." The Major swirled the brandy around in his glass, and it clung to the sides before trickling down again, flashing bright amber in the light of the fire. "She was unhappy, her marriage didn't turn out as she'd hoped, you see. She'd wanted a family and when it didn't happen things changed. Fault on both sides, I suspect. Julia and I talked a lot. I suppose I just liked her company and I believe she liked mine. She reminded me of Christine in many ways. Yes, we flirted with each other, it was in both of our natures to seek attention, but on a one-to-one level she was vulnerable, and I certainly didn't take advantage of that."

Hearing the Major's words touched Penny, considering the character bashing Julia had received from other quarters since her death. It was easy to think of Julia as an evil cartoon caricature, but everyone had their own complexities, a mixture of good and bad, and Penny's policy was to never judge anyone without having first walked in their shoes. But of one thing Penny was sure, Major Colton hadn't killed Julia. His words were tinged with kindness and respect, his demeanour solemn and truthful and he was genuinely sorry for her loss. Whether or not he and Julia had been intimate, Penny could not tell, and nor did she care.

"Did Julia have other lovers, do you think?" Mr Kelly asked the Major, who shrugged.

"Possibly, it was never discussed, but if she did I suspect they were of little consequence. Julia loved her husband." The Major was emphatic. "And from what she told me, I believe he loved her too. I just hope he didn't murder her to prove it."

# Thirteen

"I enjoyed these books very much, Penny. Thank you for the recommendations. Especially that one." Gina Hopkins handed several books to Penny and nodded to the one on the top. "About the woman who was completely fine? It was very funny, although she did drink rather a lot of vodka. I prefer gin myself, although not in those quantities. Now, I wanted to ask a favour, if I may?"

Penny placed the books in the pile of returns that she had yet to sort and turned back to Gina. A friend of her mother's, Gina had been widowed earlier in the year, and ever since had been a regular visitor to the mobile library when it stopped in Hambleton Chase. She had confided to Penny that when her husband was alive she had never read much, preferring to knit while he smoked his pipe by the fireside. Such was Gina's shock when he had keeled over from a heart attack one sunny evening in June, she had not knitted a single stitch since. "I don't think I'll ever be able to lift my needles again," Gina had said sadly. "Not with Toby's empty chair staring back at me."

Today, she was pleased to note Gina looked more like her usual self. After several months of not caring about her appearance, the older woman's hair was washed and set and the dusting of powder on her face warmed her complexion. Penny had witnessed enough library customers experiencing bereavements to know Gina still had a long way to go before settling into a new sort of normalcy, but she seemed to have turned a corner.

"Of course," Penny answered. "How can I help?"

"I know the borrowing limit is three books at a time, but I wondered if an exception would be possible, just to see me through Christmas?" Gina wrung her hands. "I'm not sure how I'll cope next week otherwise. You won't be coming around in the library van, will you?"

Penny considered the request. Due to the small supply of books she was able to carry in the van, it was necessary to keep the borrowing limit low, and even then she sometimes had to restock before Thursdays, the day she took the van to the main library at Winstoke. If the reading matter was not regularly rotated, she faced an outcry from the regulars. She manually selected books to fulfil whatever requests she had received that week, as well as trying to introduce enough new material to keep everyone else happy whilst ensuring a few old favourites were always close at hand.

"I'm off all next week Gina, but I'll see what I can do. How many did you have in mind?" In Winstoke the borrowing limit was five books per person, for a maximum of twenty-one days at a time, not that Gina would have them on loan for that long.

"Would six be all right? Otherwise it's just me, the telly, and a bottle of gin, and there's only so many times I can watch Mary Poppins or The Wizard of Oz before I go crazy."

"Six is fine, as long as you don't tell anyone. Let it be our secret." Penny winced at her choice of words. She was already keeping far too many secrets than she was comfortable with.

Gina smiled, "Thank you, Penny. I really appreciate it. I've been dreading staring at the four walls for days on end while everything's closed. Marianne and her family will call me on Christmas morning, of course, but their Christmas Day will be almost over by the time I get up. They're doing something ridiculous like having a barbecue on the beach." She frowned, "They don't go to church either. I'm afraid my grandchildren are heathens!"

Gina's only daughter lived in Australia and Penny's mother had mentioned she wasn't coming home for Christmas, due to having made an extended trip when her father had died. "I'm sure they're good children, that's the main thing," Penny said with diplomacy. Religion and politics were subjects she avoided. Except for the occasional conversation with her father at election time, she kept her own counsel on both, having witnessed close to home how the alternative led to arguments, and even violence on one occasion. That incident resulted in a bloody nose and a case of wounded pride for those involved, as well as a lifetime ban from the library van. Penny hoped it sent an important message to the community, she and all library patrons were to be treated with respect.

Gina had begun to browse the latest selection of legal thrillers when Susie's familiar face appeared at the back of the van, grinning like the Cheshire Cat.

"I was lured by the sweets," Susie said, holding up a chocolate-covered caramel. "Can anyone just help themselves?" She stuffed the sweet into her mouth without waiting for Penny to reply.

Penny climbed out of the van. "What brings you to Hambleton Chase? Don't tell me it was my tin of Christmas sweets." She peered into the container hung up on the door out of Fischer's reach, and found it almost empty. The library customers weren't shy about helping themselves to freebies, that was for sure.

Susie shook her head and swallowed, "It's the Hambleton Ramblers' prize-giving this afternoon. The Rambler of the Year Award is a feature worthy of the front page of the Gazette's Christmas edition. I'm helping out as one of the reporters called in sick, although I think it's a case of hangoveritis. I can't stay long, just wanted to pop over and see how things are going." She took a step back from the van and Penny followed suit, closing the gap between them.

"So, how's the investigation going?" Susie asked in hushed tones.

Penny sighed, "It's not what I was expecting. It seems to happen much easier in the books I read. All I've managed to achieve so far is to rake through people's private lives and unearth their secrets. It's all a bit sordid to be honest. There's certainly been no official breakthrough yet, but we are following some interesting lines of inquiry, as the saying goes. But I probably shouldn't be discussing it without speaking to Inspector Monroe first."

"Don't worry, Penny, I'm not asking you to compromise yourself or the investigation. I can keep my mouth shut you know that. But can I ask you a favour?"

"You can ask, but I can't promise anything, Susie. Although you know I'll help if I can."

"All I want is first dibs on the story when it breaks. I may not have a degree but I'm a good writer, Penny, and if I can get an exclusive on this one it could mean a promotion, doing the job I love."

"It's fine with me. I can't see a problem, although I'll need to run it passed Inspector Monroe. Once the murderer has been caught the story will be reported on anyway, and I'd rather you do it than anyone else."

"Thanks so much. You're a great friend," Susie said, giving her a hug.

At the sound of approaching footsteps and a polite cough they turned.

"Hello, Penny."

Penny's heart skipped a beat at the steel grey eyes staring back at her, her mind going completely blank. She was glad when Susie stepped forward, her friend's curiosity hiding Penny's embarrassment at being rendered momentarily speechless.

"Hello, I'm Susie Hughes," she said, holding out her hand. "And you are…?"

"Detective Inspector John Monroe," he shook Susie's hand. "It's nice to meet you, Mrs Hughes. I've been meaning to have a word with you actually, about the Julia Wargraves case. Perhaps we could speak in a minute or two? I just wanted to ask Penny something first, if you don't mind."

"Not at all," Susie said, giving Penny a look reminiscent of their schooldays when they were in trouble with a teacher for some minor mis-demeanour or other. Penny tried to keep a straight face as Susie turned and climbed into the van, grabbing another sweet from the tin as she did so.

"I'm glad I bumped into you, Penny. I was in the area in connection with the Wargraves case, and I saw the van. While I'm here, I was wondering if I could join the library?"

"Of course, Inspector. I'll just get you a form. Won't be a moment." Penny entered the van, where Susie met her with a smirk. Gina Hopkins was still there, now perusing the row of medical thrillers.

"He's a sight for sore eyes," Susie whispered, as Penny

tried to find a library application form in her admin folder. "You never said."

"Can't say I noticed."

"That's not why you're all flustered, then?" Susie grinned. "I wonder why he doesn't just join the library in Winstoke? It's a stone's throw from the police station."

"Ssh, he'll hear you!" Penny hissed, grabbing a form. "And how old are you anyway, twelve?"

Susie laughed raucously as Penny exited the van.

"Here you are, Inspector," Penny handed him the form. "If you leave it at Winstoke library when it's completed, Emma will issue you with a library card."

Inspector Monroe folded the form and placed it in the inside pocket of his overcoat. "Maybe if I have it completed by tomorrow, I could give it to you then? I was hoping we could meet to catch up on the investigation. If you can't make it to the station, I can come to you in Holt's End or Thistle Grange. Your call."

"I'll come to the station," Penny replied, wondering how he knew the library's whereabouts on a Wednesday. For that matter, had he known in advance she would be in Hambleton Chase today?

"I'll look forward to it," Fischer had appeared at the Inspector's heels, tail wagging exuberantly at the sound of a familiar friendly voice, and he reached down to stroke him. "See you tomorrow, Fischer. Bye, Penny. If you'll excuse me, I'll just have a word with Mrs Hughes before I leave."

"Of course. I'll get her."

Inside the van Susie was pretending to be engrossed in a book, even though Penny would have bet money on her having listened to every word. Especially when she saw the title of the book Susie held; Needlecraft for beginners. Susie wouldn't know one end of a needle from the other.

"Are you done?" Susie snapped the book shut and returned it to the shelf. "I'll call you later. Bye," and in typical Susie fashion, she rushed out.

Penny turned to Gina Hopkins, who was holding an armful of books, and smiled. "I hope I didn't keep you waiting, Gina. Let's get these checked out for you."

As it happened, Penny missed Susie's call that evening, due to a red sports car parked outside when she arrived home. The car's lights were on and judging from the plumes coming from the exhaust, the engine was running. When she and Fischer got out of the van she recognised Ruth Lacey sitting in the driver's seat.

Ruth's car door slammed, and she scurried up the path, "Penny? Do you have a minute?"

Up close, Penny could see Ruth was drawn, her face etched with worry. She unlocked the front door and stood aside, "Come in," she said, turning on the lights. "Can I take your coat?"

Ruth shook her head, "It's fine. I don't want to keep you. It's just..." Her expression faltered, and Penny hung her own coat on the peg in the hallway before ushering Ruth into the living room. The room was warm, embers from that morning's fire still glowing in the stove, and she added a couple of logs as Ruth slumped onto the sofa. She sat in the armchair Edward preferred, as it had the best view of the television, and Fischer settled in his dog bed, tired after most of the day spent outdoors in Hambleton Chase.

"I wanted to apologise again about Sunday," Ruth began, setting her handbag on the floor. "You must think I'm dreadful."

"Don't worry about it."

Ruth stared at her, "No, there's something I need to get off my chest. As if getting drunk wasn't bad enough, my gossiping about Stanley and Julia was out of order. When I woke up yesterday morning I remembered our conversation, and I've been feeling sick about it ever since."

"Why is that?"

"I think you might have got the wrong end of the stick. I'm aware you've been helping the police with their inquiries ever since you handed in that bottle of cordial Julia was drinking the night she died. I saw for myself how chummy you were with Inspector Monroe when he came over to the table to speak to you. I wouldn't want you to think I was involved in any way, that's all."

Penny decided to say as little as possible and leave the talking to Ruth. "I'm not sure what you mean. Involved in what, exactly?"

"Julia's murder. I couldn't stand the woman, but I didn't kill her, just in case you were thinking I did."

"Why would I think that?"

Ruth's face hardened, "I'm not sure what sort of game you're playing, Penny, but there's no point acting dumb. I know you know about me and Stanley."

*I do now*, Penny thought to herself. To Ruth, she said, "About your affair?"

Ruth averted her eyes, confirming what Penny had suspected all along.

Penny sighed, "It's none of my business, Ruth, but I wish I didn't know, because it puts me in a difficult position given that Edward and Mark are friends."

At that point Ruth looked up, her eyes meeting Penny's. "I'd appreciate if you didn't say anything to Edward or my husband. I'd like to deal with it in private with Mark."

"I wasn't intending to," Penny replied. "I'm more interested in what you were saying on Sunday about Julia, and how you thought Stanley would be happier if she was out of the way. What did you mean by that?"

Ruth gazed down at Fischer and was quiet for so long Penny wondered if she had heard her. Finally, Ruth replied in a weary tone, "I wanted Julia out of the picture as well, I admit it. I thought with her off the scene Stanley and

I would be free to be together. I'm ashamed to say I said to Stanley, only in jest you understand? that it would be easier if Julia was dead. So I suppose indirectly it's my fault for putting the idea into his head in the first place. But I didn't mean for him to murder her, Penny." Her eyes filled with tears. "I just meant that his divorce would be messy, you know? Julia would have taken him to the cleaners."

"I'm not sure I'm following you, Ruth. What makes you think Stanley killed his wife? Did he tell you as much?"

Penny held her breath for Ruth's response.

"He patted my hand and said not to worry, he was taking care of everything. But the strange thing is, now Julia's gone he's been acting distant with me. I guess that's his guilt kicking in." Ruth's chin wobbled. "I've made a terrible mistake, I realise that now. If there's any way I can save my marriage, that's my priority. Visiting Stanley in prison for the next twenty years certainly isn't."

"I see. You'll have to tell this to Inspector Monroe, Ruth, you know that, don't you?"

Ruth sniffed, "Yes. And my relationship with Stanley will be paraded at his trial. I just came here to ask if you could at least give me until tomorrow to speak to Mark before I go to the police? I owe my husband the courtesy to hear it from me first."

"Of course."

Ruth stood up and reached for her bag, "Thank you." She gave Penny a curt nod. "Don't get up, I'll see myself out."

Penny remained seated until she heard Ruth's footsteps in the hallway and the front door slam shut. Then she spoke to Fischer, who had opened one eye, "Come on, little Fish Face, I'll get your dinner, and I think I need a strong cup of tea."

## FOURTEEN

Penny decided that calling into the Police Station after she finished work at five the following evening, would allow Ruth Lacey a generous amount of time to speak to both her husband and Inspector Monroe. If Ruth hadn't done so by then it would be out of Penny's hands. She telephoned Mr Kelly on her way to work to give him an update and ask if he wanted to come along. "I can pick you up on my way to Winstoke?" she suggested.

"I would, Penny, but it's the Christmas Show at Cherrytree Downs Primary School, and my granddaughter's singing so I can't miss it. You don't mind going by yourself do you? Please, give my regards to Inspector Monroe. And if what Ruth says is true, I have to say I'm very disappointed in Stanley."

"You and me both, Mr Kelly. Anyway, enjoy the show, and I'll let you know how it goes."

When she caught up with Edward to let him know about the change of plans for the evening, he wasn't quite as accommodating. "What do you mean you can't meet me straight after work? Honestly, Penny, that's twice this week you've let me down, and you know I need your help to finish my

Christmas shopping. What are my family going to think when I turn up sans gifts?"

"I didn't say I couldn't come shopping with you, Edward, just that I'm not sure what time I'll be finished at the Police Station," Penny said, trying to keep her voice calm. "The shops will be open late, so it shouldn't be a problem." Reminding Edward that yet again, he shouldn't have left his shopping for presents until the last minute. He had several nieces and nephews he was happy to lavish gifts on, but no clue what to buy. Not that Penny did either, but by asking people with children or grandchildren in a similar age group, she was able to work it out. Either this method had escaped Edward, or he was happy to leave it to her. She suspected the latter.

"Fine," he said, in an exaggerated tone that suggested the opposite. "Call me when you've finished with Monroe, and I'll come and meet you at the Police Station. I don't want you walking to my office by yourself. Parking's a nightmare and there are far too many drunks lurching around the streets this time of year."

"All right," Penny said, before hanging up, relieved she didn't have to speak to him anymore. Edward was becoming far too moody and demanding for her liking.

Penny was surprised to see Inspector Monroe waiting when she pulled up in her usual spot in Thistle Grange around lunchtime. When she opened the door Fischer jumped out of the van, and after a quick greeting with the policeman bounded over to where his friends Gatsby and Daisy were standing waiting with their owner Mr Sheridan. Penny waved them off before turning to the Inspector, who was watching her with a serious expression.

"My car is parked across the road," he said stepping off the pavement. "Let's get out of the cold, I need to talk to you."

They headed towards a black land-rover in silence, where he opened the passenger door for her, and waited until she was settled before opening the driver's side and climbing in himself.

"I hope I haven't alarmed you, Penny. I know you said you would call by the station later, but I had a couple of visitors this morning, and things have moved on. I wanted to save you making a wasted trip."

"A *couple* of visitors?"

"Yes, Ruth Lacey was accompanied by her husband, Mark. She was very cooperative and explained she had spoken to you yesterday evening." He frowned, "Which you ought to have informed me about, by the way."

"I gave Ruth my word, on the understanding she would come and tell you everything after she had spoken with her husband. She obviously kept her promise." Penny watched his face twitch. "I also didn't think Stanley was in any danger of absconding, considering his wife's funeral is in a couple of days. What happens now?"

"Stanley will be brought in for questioning. Depending on what happens, he may be arrested and charged. He'll need a good lawyer if so."

"I see." Penny averted her gaze to where Mr Sheridan, Fischer and the two black lab puppies were crossing the road in the direction of the woods.

"Is something bothering you, Penny?"

Penny wasn't surprised by the Inspector's question. His eyes had never left her and the turmoil in her mind probably showed on her face.

"Yes, actually there is. It's difficult to explain but I just have a feeling something's not right. What do you call it in your line of work, a hunch?"

Monroe laughed, "Only if I'm prepared to get my marching orders. I'm afraid it was books and TV that made that misguided notion popular."

"So what would you call it then?"

"Hard work, diligence, experience and a possible dash of intuition. It helps if you understand people and have some local knowledge though, which is, I suspect, where you're getting this feeling from."

"Doesn't quite roll off the tongue though does it?" Penny said with a smile. "I suppose it's intuition in that case. So far all we've managed to unearth are pieces of gossip and extra-material affairs."

"Ah, the sordid underbelly of English village life you mean?"

Now it was Penny's turn to laugh, "Well that's a bit melodramatic, but you get the gist."

"It's all part of the local colour."

"Well, from where I'm sitting the local colour appears to be just varying shades of green."

Monroe nodded, "Envy and avarice. They're basic motives for murder."

Penny sighed, "Yes, I suppose they are. But what if we're wrong about Stanley? All we have is Ruth's word, and considering the relationship has cooled off, this could be her way of exacting revenge. Or maybe she did it and is trying to pin it on Stanley, or maybe they're in it together and are trying to attach the blame to the each other now their affair is out in the open. We can't know how Stanley will react until we speak to him of course, but I'd very much like to talk to him at home before he's officially taken to the police station. Would that be possible?"

There was a long pause before the Inspector spoke, "Explain your reasons to me, Penny."

She glanced at him, wondering if he was being serious. He was.

"Go on," he encouraged. "I'd welcome your insight."

"Well, like I said before, we only have Ruth's word for it, and she isn't an impartial witness. I also feel sorry for Stanley, an emotional response I know, but the poor man has just lost his wife in dreadful circumstances, and if he's innocent then taking him in officially will only add fuel to the fire. There will always be a stigma attached to him after that and the gossip will run wild. I don't think that's fair to do at this stage because we really don't have any proof. I think we should show a little compassion."

"Succinctly put. Let me think it over while I grab us some coffee. My caffeine levels are dangerously low. Do you have time before you have to get back to work?"

Penny checked her watch, even though she knew she had plenty of time to spare before opening the van for the afternoon session. In any case, she could see any library customers arriving from where they were parked. "Yes, all right," she said, replying with a smile. "Except, I'd like a tea, if you don't mind. There's a little cafe on Cobblers Lane, they do hot drinks to take away…"

"The Pot and Kettle?" Inspector Monroe already had his hand on the door handle. "I know it. Stay here and keep warm, I'll be right back."

A flurry of snow had started up, and Penny was glad to sit back and wait in the comfort of the car, although she didn't have to wait long as Inspector Monroe returned in record time. She idly wondered if he had pulled rank and skipped the queue. He handed Penny her tea in a lidded cardboard cup, and placed his coffee in the drinks holder.

"Thank you," she said, gratefully taking the cup and warming her hands.

He opened a white paper bag and held it towards her, "Mince pie? They're warm."

"Yes please. I'm trying to cut down on the sweet stuff, but I have absolutely no willpower." She reached into the bag and pulled out a sugar-dusted pastry encased in thick silver foil. "Are you going home for Christmas?" she asked him, between bites.

"Assuming the case is wrapped up by then, yes," he said, taking a mouthful of coffee and sighing appreciatively. "I'm from the Peak District originally and my family is still up there. There'll be ten of us crammed into my parents' little house for Christmas dinner. My sisters are both married, and their children are at the really fun age where Christmas is magical. What about you?"

"I'm going to my parents' too. Susie, who you met yesterday, is joining us along with her two children. Usually it's just me and my parents, so this year we're making it quite a crowd. I'm really looking forward to it."

"No Edward?"

Penny shook her head. She willed her cheeks not to flush and for once, they obeyed. "We decided it was easier to each visit our own family, rather than try and do two dinners in one day or take alternate years."

"Your parents owned the bookshop in Winstoke before they retired didn't they? I was in there recently and liked it very much. The owner was a bit pushy, but he carries a good selection of books. I picked up one by an errant, real life ex-head-of-state, whose literary alter ego goes missing. That should see me through the train journey up North and back."

Penny was relieved the spotlight was off her and Edward and the conversation had turned to more neutral ground. "I've read it, so I won't reveal any spoilers. We have it in the library, you know. Which reminds me, do you have your application form, and I'll hand it in for you when I'm at the main library tomorrow?"

"Yes, I do." He reached inside his coat and handed her the folded form.

"Thanks." Penny held the form in her hand, feeling suddenly self-conscious. "I should be going now, I can see a queue starting to form at the van. Thanks for the tea and mince-pie. Have you decided?"

Inspector Monroe gave her a blank look, clearly confused.

"Whether I can come with you to speak to Stanley? I think he'll respond better if I'm there to be honest, as he knows me."

"Oh yes, I think that will be fine, providing you let me lead the questioning. It's an official visit. Are you free to go this afternoon or does it need to be this evening?"

"This evening would be better. I don't want to let the people here down, because the library won't be back after today due to the Christmas break."

"All right we'll wait until later. I doubt Ruth will tip him off, but just in case I've got someone watching the house. I'll pick you up at the green in Cherrytree Downs at seven o' clock and we can go together, how does that sound?"

It sounded like Penny was going to have to let Edward down again, despite her assurances to him earlier.

"That's fine," she said, opening the car door. "Although I'd like to walk over with Fischer, it's not far from the village green."

"All right, a walk it is."

"Great, I'll see you then."

# FIFTEEN

"Hello, Mr Wargraves, it's DI Monroe. You already know Miss Finch, I believe? I just have a few more questions for you, if that's all right?" Without waiting for an answer, Inspector Monroe wiped his feet on the sisal mat in the porch and took a step up into Stanley's hallway.

"Stay there, Fischer, we won't be long," Penny said, as she watched the little dog settle in a corner, looking thoroughly dejected. She followed the Inspector into the house.

Stanley closed the door behind them and let out a sigh. "Yes, do come in."

He directed them into the kitchen and cleared some dirty dishes from the wooden dining table to one of the marble counter tops, already strewn with unwashed plates smeared in ketchup, boxes of breakfast cereals and crumbs from the toaster.

"Sorry about the mess," he mumbled, pulling out a chair. "Ruth's let me down. She was supposed to be organising a cleaner. I'd offer you refreshments but I don't think there are any clean cups. Or fresh milk, come to think of it."

"That's all right, Mr Wargraves." Inspector Monroe gazed around the kitchen before moving a newspaper off the chair at the end of the table and sitting down. "I'm sure doing the dishes isn't high priority for you at the moment."

"Have you been eating properly, Stanley?" Penny asked, as she took a seat next to him. She watched as he rubbed his unshaven chin. His reddened skin had a dull tinge to it and his clothes and hair were dishevelled and unwashed.

"People have been very kind, leaving casseroles and pies," Stanley said. "I really must return their dishes, once I get this place cleaned up." He turned to Penny. "I don't suppose you know anyone who might like to earn a bit of extra money until I get proper help? The smallest things seem impossible right now. Ruth resigning this morning was the final blow."

Penny looked across to Inspector Monroe, who gave her a silent nod, which she took as permission to speak. He obviously realised Stanley was likely to be more forthcoming with her, official visit or not.

"Ruth resigned? I'm sorry to hear that, Stanley."

Stanley gave her a sad smile, "It's for the best, Penny, truth be told. I've done some things I'm not proud of but having an affair with Ruth was the worst of them," He gave Inspector Monroe a sideways look. "Ruth called me this morning. She said her resignation letter is in the post and she wouldn't be working her notice. Not that I blame her, of course. She wished me well and said she hoped the judge would be lenient. That's when I realised she really believed I killed Julia. Either that or it's part of her plan to let me be the fall guy. God, what a mess."

Inspector Monroe's face was blank when he asked, "Did you kill your wife, Mr Wargraves?"

"Don't be ridiculous," Stanley's jaw was set. "If there wasn't a lady present, I'd put it a lot stronger than that. Anyway, as soon as I saw one of your chaps stationed in the car across the street all day, I figured you'd be around. I've primed my lawyer, so if you're taking me in say so and I'll make the call."

"I had to ask Mr Wargraves, it's my job. But if you've got something to get off your chest, go right ahead and call your lawyer."

Stanley slammed his fist on the table, "Stop trying to call my bluff! I've got nothing to hide, don't you see?" He turned to Penny with a beseeching look, and his voice finally cracked when he spoke again. "My beautiful Julia isn't coming back. I adored her and all I ever wanted was for her to find it in her heart to forgive me for letting her down, and now it's too late. Nothing matters without her."

Penny leaned towards him, her voice soft, "You let her down by having an affair? Did Julia know about Ruth?"

Stanley hung his head and gave a shaky sigh, "I believe so," he said at last, looking up. "But that's not what I meant. I suppose I may as well you, I've nothing left to lose."

"When Julia and I got married all we ever wanted was a family, but no matter how much we tried it never happened. Eventually we sought medical help and after a battery of tests the results came back. Julia was fine, but I wasn't. We would never be able to have children of our own and it was all my fault. It was back when we didn't have much money. I had just started the business and IVF wasn't an option, we just couldn't afford it in those days. We considered adoption but there was a huge waiting list and the likelihood of a baby was rare. Eventually as time passed, even though we never spoke of it, we both just gave up."

"I'm sorry," Penny murmured, remembering Major Colton's assessment of Julia's unhappiness. She wondered if Julia had known how hard it had been on Stanley too.

"We just soldiered on," Stanley continued. "I suppose we each of us dealt with it in different ways. I threw myself into work, with the result that the business was a great success. Ironically, by the time we could afford IVF our age was against us. Instead, I lavished Julia with gifts and holidays and designer clothes. Whatever she wanted she got. But fripperies were no substitute for what she had longed for most, a child. The more she pulled away from me, the more I despaired."

Penny's eyes sought out Stanley's bloodshot ones, "Is that when you started seeing Ruth?"

He swallowed, "I resisted for a long time, but Ruth was

very persistent, and was quick to point out Julia wasn't very respectful in the way she treated me. Julia had several… let's call them friendships. I like to believe they provided her with nothing more than shoulders to cry on, although I'll never know for sure. Ruth was convinced I was deluding myself. The more she pursued me the more I opened up to the possibility of happiness with another woman. For a while there, I truly believed Julia and I would be better off without each other. Thankfully, I came to my senses."

"Ruth came to see me last night and told me you said you'd take care of everything when it came to Julia. What did you mean by that?"

Stanley buried his face in his palms and rocked his upper body. Penny could see Inspector Monroe observe his every movement, his expression remaining impassive. He indicated to Penny to remain quiet, so she waited for Stanley to speak. When he removed his hands from his face his skin was blotchy, and tears rolled down his cheeks.

"Excuse a foolish man his selfish ways, Penny. A couple of weeks ago Julia and I sat down and talked properly for the first time in years. Things had come to a head with Ruth, or should I say a heady passion, and she gave me an ultimatum pushing me to leave Julia. It was make-or-break time for Julia and I." He paused, wiping his eyes with his sleeve. "To cut a long story short, we had a heart-to-heart and got a lot of things off our chests. Resentment and misunderstandings fester, and picking the scabs off old wounds is a painful thing to do. We decided, after a lot of tears and recriminations on both sides, to put the past behind us and give our marriage another try. I hadn't quite got around to calling things off with Ruth, and then... " His voice trailed off.

Penny finished his sentence, "Julia died?"

Stanley nodded. "Ruth couldn't understand why I wasn't happy about it. She thought it's what I wanted you see, to be free to be with her but she was wrong. At one point it even crossed my mind Ruth might have spiked Julia's drink. The truth is Julia always had my heart, and never more so than now. To my shame I pushed Ruth away without giving her a proper explanation. She at least deserved that much."

Penny wasn't sure she agreed with Stanley's assessment of Ruth, but she refrained from passing comment.

Inspector Monroe, quiet and observant during the visit, now spoke up, "I think that's all we need from you for now, Mr Wargraves. Thank you for being so candid with us, and once again I'm sorry for your loss. Penny and I will get out of your way now."

Penny scrambled to her feet, torn between doing what Inspector Monroe had stated, and offering to stay and clean Stanley's kitchen. She decided that going against Inspector Monroe was probably unwise, and instead added, "I'll ask around if anyone can spare a few hours to come in and clean, Stanley. I'm sure we'll get something organised for you."

Stanley stared at them, relief relaxing his features, "You're not taking me to the station?"

Inspector Monroe was gruff, but not rude, "No, that won't be necessary at the moment." He motioned to Penny. "Fischer will be wondering where you've got to. Ready?"

Penny nodded and turned to Stanley, "Bye, Stanley. Don't get up. I'm sorry I won't be able to come to the funeral tomorrow, but I'll be thinking of you. Is there anyone I can call to keep you company tonight?"

Stanley gave her a tight smile, a lone tear trickling down his face and shook his head. "No, there's no one. But I'll be all right, Penny, don't worry about me. I prefer to be alone."

Outside in the porch Penny looked up at Inspector Monroe after he had closed the front door, "Well?"

Inspector Monroe smiled, "I think you made a good call to question Stanley here, rather than at the station."

"So you don't think he killed Julia?"

"I didn't say that. He made a good case and from what I could see was telling the truth. However, so did Ruth Lacey. Until we've got proof one way or another, I'm keeping an open mind. Now, I'll just go over and tell my man across the road he can go. If you wait, I'll walk you home."

"Come on, Fischer," Penny said, reaching down to grab his lead. "It looks like we need to find you a tree. I'm sure Stanley won't mind if you use one of his." She led him down the steps and cut across the snow covered lawn to the walled boundary of the garden, which was lined with a neat row of evergreen trees. While Fischer cocked his leg, Penny peered over the wall into Mrs Duke's garden next door. It didn't have as many plants or shrubs as Julia's prize-winning showpiece, but from what she could see it was well-kept. She spied a small upright stone in one corner illuminated by the outside light, and realised with a start it was a grave. Footsteps crunched across the snow, and she turned expecting to see Inspector Monroe, but to her surprise it was Stanley.

"I thought that was you out here," he said to her, smiling down at Fischer. "I just wanted to say thanks for coming along with Inspector Monroe tonight. I have a feeling if you hadn't been there, the conversation may have got heated. I'd probably be in a cell right now for having assaulted a police officer."

Penny smiled, "You're welcome. Inspector Monroe's bark's worse than his bite, but don't tell him I said so. What's that over there, by the way?" She pointed to the stone beside Mrs Duke's shed.

Stanley rolled his eyes, "It's a grave for Mrs Duke's cat. Julia hated it," he chuckled. "Anyway, when the cat was run over by a car, Mrs Duke was very upset. She accused Julia of killing it of course, even though we were away at the time. They buried the hatchet in the end, once Mrs Duke came to her senses. She's been civil since then, if not exactly friendly."

"Losing a much loved pet must be hard. If anything happened to Fischer I'd be absolutely devastated." Penny glanced down the path to where Inspector Monroe was waiting for her, the mist from his breath visible in the cold night air, and tugged Fischer's lead. "Good night, Stanley."

"Good night, Penny. And thanks again."

# SIXTEEN

Penny's hopes for her last day at work before Christmas, to be a laid back, mince-pie eating, jolly Christmas jumper sort of affair were dashed early on, when Fischer failed to greet her that morning from his customary position at the foot of the stairs.

"Fischer? Where are you little man?" She dashed to the lounge where she found him still laid in his bed, sad eyes looking up at her, and a suspicious pile of vomit laced with grass on the rug. His tail gave a single thump as she felt his nose. It was warm and dry.

"Aw, poor Fischer," she said. "Have you got an upset tummy? Did you eat something nasty in the woods yesterday?" She gently stroked his head. "Let's get cleaned up, and then we'll take a trip to The Rough Spot."

The Rough Spot was the veterinary clinic in Cherrytree Downs. The name had started as a joke by the locals due to the catch-phrase used by the vet, but it had persisted and eventually renamed officially. The logo was a cartoon-style Dalmatian dog with one of his black spots coloured red.

Fischer's lethargy had dissipated by the time she was ready to leave the house, and he had drunk plenty of water. But he had refused his breakfast, and couldn't even be enticed by a treat. "Well you seem a little brighter, but you're not one hundred percent. It's best we get you checked out just in case, okay?" When she lifted her keys, his cue to dash to the door, he instead took a sedate walk and waited patiently for Penny.

Opening the front door, a blanket of deep, fresh snow greeted them. "I'd better carry you to the vet's otherwise you'll disappear. It's just as well we don't need to move the van today."

Thursday was a no-travel morning for the library van, as it was stationed in Cherrytree Downs until the afternoon, when Penny drove to Winstoke to restock for the following week. As there would be no mobile library service until the New Year due to the holiday, the heavy snow meant the restocking would have to wait. And if she wasn't able to move the van to its usual spot beside the green, it wouldn't be too much of a problem, she could still operate where it was parked, right outside her house. When the van didn't appear at its official spot, that would be where people would come looking for her.

A 'Closed' sign was hanging inside the glass panel of the door to the surgery when Penny and Fischer arrived, but the lights in the building were on. Penny rapped three times and waited. She could hear the sound of footsteps on the tiled floor and a young man appeared, moving the cardboard sign out of the way to see who it was. Penny raised Fischer into full view and put her head close to the glass, "Is Dr Jones available?"

The young man nodded, then indicated for her to wait. He disappeared from view and a second later a man with grey hair and spectacles peered through the glass. He smiled at Penny in recognition and unlocked the door, holding it open for her to enter.

"Hello, Penny. I've not seen you for a while. I owe you some money for my books being late, don't I? I can never remember where I put them most of the time, never mind get around to reading them. I'll just get my wallet and we can settle up."

Penny shook her head, "Actually, it's not about your books, Dr Jones. I don't have an appointment, but Fischer was sick last night. I wonder if you could have a quick look at him and see what you think?"

Dr Jones reached out and gently lifted Fischer's chin, "Going through a bit of a rough spot are you, boy? Well, we can't have that." He looked at Penny, "Come on through to the examination room and I'll have a look."

After popping him on the stainless steel table, Penny sat on a wooden chair while Dr Jones examined Fischer. He gave him a thorough checkup, including his eyes, teeth, ears and stomach, and much to Fischer's surprise, his temperature.

"Has he been sick before, or was it just the once?"

"Just the once as far as I know."

"Where did he go yesterday?"

"To the woods with Gatsby and Daisy."

"Well it doesn't seem to be anything serious, and he's vomited up whatever he ate, which is a good sign. It was probably fox scat or a dead bird. Make sure he has bland food for the next few days, boiled rice and chicken is your best bet, smaller portions but more often. He'll let you know when he's ready to eat normally. It's unlikely it will happen again, but if you're concerned at all come and see me, I'm on call over the Christmas period. It's handy living next door. Now, if you go and see Michael he'll get your bill ready."

"Thank you so much. That's such a relief." Penny lifted Fischer from the table where he immediately made a beeline for a poster with a picture of cat, and began to growl softly.

"He seems more like himself already."

"I'm sure there's nothing to worry about. He'll be as right as rain before you know it."

Staring at the poster Penny was struck by a sudden thought, "Actually, Dr Jones, I wonder if you spare me a bit more time?"

"Do you remember when Mrs Duke's cat died? I'm not sure when it was, exactly."

Dr Jones raised his eyebrows, "I do, as a matter of fact. It was my birthday, twenty-fifth of August. It was one of the more memorable days since I opened the surgery."

"Why was that?"

"Mrs Duke was frantic. When she brought her cat in it was already dead. It had been run over by a car. The animal was quite a mess as you can imagine, and she was carrying it in her bare hands." He sighed. "I wasn't sure what she expected us to do, and it was a while before she calmed down enough to tell us. As it turned out she was quite rational in her request."

"What do you mean?"

"She insisted we perform a necropsy, and the subsequent results uncovered something that may have been related to the cat's demise, although it was tenuous." He frowned, "Let me consult my notes." He walked over to his laptop and after tapping a few keys turned back to Penny. "There were traces of pesticide in the cat's system, enough to potentially have been fatal. Mrs Duke wanted to know if it was possible the cat had been run over after it was already dead. An interesting theory."

"I'm confused. You mean, someone put a dead cat on the road?"

"That's what Mrs Duke seemed to think. It was possible of course, but a more plausible explanation, which I put to Mrs Duke, was the cat had been overcome while crossing, didn't make it to the other side and collapsed. Whereby a passing car mowed over it."

Penny got up and called Fischer over to attach his lead.

"How would a cat get poisoned by pesticide, was it deliberate do you think?" It still didn't make sense why Mrs Duke thought Julia responsible, especially as Julia was away at the time.

Dr Jones walked her and Fischer to the door of his consulting room, which had remained open during their visit. "Again, not conclusive. The animal could have come into contact with it in a garden or outhouse. Rat poison is commonly used around these parts. If that's what happened it's very unfortunate, but not necessarily deliberate. Pet owners tend to be careful about things like that, but other people wouldn't necessarily know. Personally I think these poisons should be banned, it's a dreadful way for any creature to die."

Penny nodded, the explanation seemed the most likely. "Poor Mrs Duke, I really empathise with her, but it sounds like it was just a terrible accident."

Dr Jones agreed. "I think she realised that in the end. Happy Christmas, Penny. Goodbye, Fischer, keep well little man."

"Happy Christmas and thanks again."

Penny approached the customer counter, where Michael had her bill ready. She took out her purse and watched him ring up the consultation fee, paying in cash. He looked familiar, but she couldn't quite place him.

"I hope you don't mind, Miss Finch," Michael said, handing over her change and lowering his voice. "I Don't have time now, we'll be open in a minute, but I wondered if I could come to the library van during my break? There's something I need to tell you."

At that moment the sound of Penny's phone buzzing in her bag rang through the reception.

“Yes of course you can," she said, wondering what he wanted to talk to her about. "Although I'll probably be parked outside my house rather than green. I don't think I can move the van now we've had all this new snow." She unzipped her bag, dropped in her purse and retrieved her phone. Waving to Michael she and Fischer left the surgery before she answered.

"Good morning, Mr Kelly."

"Good morning, Penny. Can you talk?"

"Yes, I'm just leaving The Rough Spot."

"Oh dear. Is Fischer all right?"

"He was sick this morning, something he picked up in the woods yesterday, but he's improved a lot. I think he'll be fine." Fischer was bounding happily through the deep snow, much more lively than he'd been first thing. "How was your granddaughter's show?"

"Marvellous. I don't know where the youngsters get their confidence from. How was your meeting with Inspector Monroe?"

"I'll fill you in on the details when I see you, but while

he's not ruled out Ruth and Stanley completely, I think the interest in them has lessened somewhat. However there's something else I've been thinking about. I don't think it will amount to anything, but I wanted to run it by you. We need to follow all leads however tenuous and the incident has cropped up in conversation more than once, so I think it merits a follow-up." She explained about the gravestone in Mrs Duke's garden, and her conversations with Stanley and Dr Jones about Mrs Duke's cat. "What do you think?"

"Hmm. It sounds like her grudge against Julia was irrational, but her cat obviously meant the world to her. With no other evidence to go on I suppose we could pay her a visit. However, there's something else I should mention which happened yesterday. It was quite unnerving."

The thought of Mr Kelly being unnerved was surprising to Penny, given her perception of him. "Go on," She said.

"Mrs Sykes was at the show last night. She was looking very well-dressed, which in itself is unusual, although explained by her purchases of Julia's clothes. But not only that, she's had her hair coloured and restyled in such a way it makes her look like Julia's clone. It only took one ill-advised comment from Maureen Bates about the walking dead, and Mrs Sykes was at Maureen's throat. There was an altercation during the interval, when Mrs Sykes declared Julia was a hideous woman who, and I quote, 'had it coming.' It really was most unpleasant."

By this point, Penny had almost reached home and could

see a group of people already assembled outside her house, waiting for the library to open. "We should probably speak to Mrs Sykes too in that case. Do you think you could let Inspector Monroe know? I'm busy tonight, but I could come with you tomorrow to visit Mrs Duke and Mrs Sykes." She had finally managed to placate Edward by promising she would go shopping with him after work that evening without fail. Although, the way things were looking she might need a snowmobile to get to Winstoke.

"That's fine, Penny. I'll ask Inspector Monroe and see what he thinks."

"Great. Thank you, Mr Kelly. Talk to you later."

# SEVENTEEN

Penny tied a length of decorative ribbon around the final gift in the stack of presents she had just finished wrapping, and carefully pulled out the loops into a wide bow. Lifting a large pair of scissors, she trimmed the frayed ends of the ribbon, before sitting back to admire her handiwork. As she did so, Fischer's nose edged along the rim of the coffee table, in an attempt to ascertain whether any of the scraps of wrapping paper, tape and ribbon strewn on top of it were edible.

"You'll have to wait until tomorrow to open your gifts, like everyone else," she declared, tidying the rubbish off the table into the waste basket. "For now, these are going under the tree."

Fisher wagged his tail as he watched her lift the packages off the table and move them under the twinkling spruce adorned with coloured glass baubles in the corner. He let out a bark, and Penny laughed. "Fine. You can have one tonight. Edward and I will be exchanging our gifts when he comes over later, so we can all have one each. But we're saving the rest until we go to see Granny and Granddad, okay?"

Perhaps sensing the negotiations were over, Fischer trotted off, leaving Penny to bend down and rearrange the gifts so Edward's was at the front. Technically, he had two from her rather than one, although she had wrapped them together. She had supplemented the envelope containing a double ticket for the Mini convention the following May, with something he could get the benefit from before then, a navy cashmere crew neck sweater. She knew he would wear it on weekends with a casual button-down shirt underneath, and it would go with his navy heritage-style quilted jacket. Hopefully, he would remember to use the delicate setting on his washing machine. The last one she had bought him hadn't even lasted a week, and ended up being too small even for Fischer to wear.

For Susie, she had curated a mini-hamper containing a variety of inexpensive items she knew her friend would like. A glossy lipstick, a bottle of bubble bath, a slab of artisan butterscotch chocolate and a CD for the car were included amongst the goodies, Susie was always complaining her children hi-jacked the play-list on car journeys. Ellen and Billy had selection boxes and a wall calendar each, and there were sheepskin slippers for both her parents. Even though they protested every year she shouldn't buy them anything, she always splashed out on items for them that were practical but good quality. That way, they couldn't say she had wasted her money.

The rest of the packages were for Fischer, the newest addition to the family. It was his first Christmas and considering the size of the pile, she conceded she'd probably gone a bit overboard. She looked over at him standing in the doorway, "I don't care if you're a little bit spoiled, because you're such a good boy aren't you, Fischer?" He charged over to meet her outstretched arms and she lifted him up for a cuddle and an automatic face wash. "You've brought so much happiness into my life these last few months, I don't know what I'd do without you." Glancing at the clock, she kissed his nose and put him down. "We'd better get going, Mr Kelly will be waiting. We have a very important mission ahead, and I'm going to need your help. I'll tell you all about it on the way."

Even though Penny and Mr Kelly had discussed their plan on the telephone that morning, butterflies fluttered in Penny's stomach when she saw him standing at the end of the lane, around the corner from Mrs Duke's house, their first stop. The footpaths had been cleared of snow the previous day and salted overnight, but the air remained bitterly cold, and Penny wore a woollen bobble hat pulled down over her ears. Any curls protruding from the bottom of the hat were wrapped under a scarf that came up as high as her nose, and her full length padded coat, gloves and boots afforded maximum protection from the elements from the neck down. If she needed to be identified in a line-up, she was confident she wouldn't be recognised, except for Fischer giving the game away. He was harder to disguise.

Mr Kelly, always well-turned-out, wore a tweed cap and a heavy overcoat, and leaned on his walking cane as she approached. His face broke into a smile. "Don't look so worried, Penny. What can possibly go wrong?"

"Mrs Duke goes crazy, bumps us off and buries our bodies with her cat?"

Mr Kelly chuckled, "If it's any consolation, she won't have time to bury us before she's caught. I'm sure if Inspector Monroe doesn't hear anything back from us by this afternoon he'll come looking for us. Although, he did say his train leaves Winstoke at four 'o clock. After that we're on our own."

"That's okay, I was hoping to be home before lunch." Penny said, relaxing slightly at Mr Kelly's composure. "Let's go through it again quickly. How long will I give you before I sneak around the back?"

"Stay out of sight like we discussed until you see me go in. I'll say I'm visiting to ask if she'll help out with the next Summer Fete fundraiser, because so many people have put her name forward. If I stroke her ego she'll be too honoured to refuse."

"Good idea."

"If she doesn't offer to put the kettle on I'll suggest it myself and keep her talking for as long as possible. That should give you and Fischer time to look in the shed and see what you can find. Got it?"

Penny nodded.

"You can text me to keep in touch if you need to. I'll ask to use the bathroom while I'm there and see if there's anything in the cabinet." He paused, frowning. "Searching her bedroom might be a bit of a stretch. I wouldn't want her to get the wrong idea if she catches me rooting through her drawers."

Penny tried to keep a straight face but failed, "You might not be able to live that one down," she laughed. "It would keep the village gossips going for months." Something else had occurred to her, but she couldn't see any way around it. "Our footprints in the snow are going to be a bit of a giveaway, but that can't be helped. We'll just have to ask for forgiveness later."

"Absolutely. Although you can always say Fischer escaped and you chased after him. We'll meet back here when we're both done, then we can repeat the process at Mrs Syke's place. I'm not sure if she has a shed, but we'll find out when we get there."

"What if something goes wrong?"

"I can't imagine it will, we don't really think Mrs Duke is involved, but if you have any worries at all just call Inspector Monroe, he said he'd come straight over if needed." Mr Kelly straightened his cap and winked at Penny. "Right, I'm going in."

"Good luck." She held her breath and watched him turn the corner, before tugging Fischer's lead and setting off at a slow pace, several steps behind. "Remember what I told you, Fischer," she said in a low voice. "Nice and quiet, okay? No barking or carrying on. This is serious stuff."

Fischer gave her a wide-eyed stare and padded along obediently beside her. When Mr Kelly opened Mrs Duke's gate, Penny crept forward far enough to watch him walk up the path and ring the doorbell, whilst making sure she she couldn't be seen from the house. The door opened and Mrs Duke appeared on the step. The sound of voices and even a laugh was audible, although she was unable to make out what was being said. The door shut with a bang, and then it went quiet.

"This is it, Fischer," Penny whispered to him, her heart pounding. She shook her arm so that her watch was visible. "We'll wait another three minutes and make a run for it."

It was the longest three minutes of her life, and she used all of her concentration to psych herself up for the quick sprint to the shed, which she estimated should not take longer than thirty seconds once she was through the gate. The hardest part would be getting past Mrs Duke's front and side windows unseen, but Mr Kelly was aware of that, and she was relying on him to divert Mrs Duke's attention long enough for her to get to the shed undiscovered. The second hand on her watch swept around the dial.

Three… two… one…

She jumped to her feet. "Let's go!"

Head bowed, she made for the gate, grateful Mr Kelly had left it unlatched so she didn't have to take her gloves off, and slipped through, Fischer close beside her. She shadowed the boundary of the garden, along the hedge at the front until it met the wall at the side. Then some sixth sense made her look up. At that exact moment, it seemed Stanley Wargraves looked straight at her from his garden next door, where he was filling the bird feeder.

There was only one thing for it. She dived flat on her face into the snow.

Fisher sniffed around her head and she scrambled onto all fours, pausing for a moment in case Stanley Wargraves looked over the wall. What on earth would she say to him? In the absence of any better ideas, she began to crawl. Gloves and knees sodden, she kept going, head down, until she was level with the shed. Easing herself onto her feet she straightened up just enough to peer over the wall. Stanley was gone. She exhaled in relief.

"That was close," she murmured, shaking some of the snow off her arms and legs.

She stepped across the grave stone for Mrs Duke's cat and leaned closer to read the engraving:

*'Miss Marmalade*

*Much loved and sorely missed*

*RIP'*

From there, it was only a few steps to the door of the shed. Taking her gloves off, she slowly slid aside the rusty bolt, thanking her lucky stars the padlock was hanging off. If she ever had to do something like this again she'd come better prepared. The door creaked open and she stepped inside. Looking around, there were the usual accoutrements essential to maintain a country garden; a petrol mower, strimmer, pruning shears, rake, several watering cans, gloves and empty plant pots. Fischer sniffed the items at floor level while Penny's eye was drawn to a solitary shelf, where an open box of grass seed was lined up beside several plastic bottles and sprays.

Weed-killer, Path cleaner, Insecticide, Headstone cleaning spray. She lifted each in turn and began to check the ingredients, her hands shaking. "I'm not sure what I'm looking for, Fischer," she said in dismay. "I'm sure all this stuff is poisonous if consumed. It's knowing whether it matches what killed Julia that's the problem. I could take photos of the bottles, and give them to Inspector Monroe, how does that sound?" It was eerily quiet. "Fischer?"

From a quick check of the shed, Fischer was nowhere to be seen. She had dropped his lead when she began to read the labels, and he'd wandered off. Penny spun around and raced outside, patting her leg with urgency. "Fischer," she whispered, her voice carried away by the wind. "Fischer, where are you?"

Suddenly she heard an excited whine and dashed to the

other side of the shed, where she found Fischer playing in a huge mound of snow.

"Ssh," she said, just loud enough to be heard, and extended her arm to grab his lead. "What did I say about keeping quiet? Come down from there, Fischer, or you're in big trouble." He ignored her still pawing frantically at the snow. "I mean it, Fischer," she hissed in desperation. "You're going to get us caught!" She glanced at the house, convinced Mrs Duke was about to come running out any second and demand an explanation. Still Fischer growled, burrowing deeper and deeper, snow flying in all directions.

With a flash of clarity, Penny suddenly realised what the mound was. Underneath the snow was a layer of straw, and below that, leaves. Fischer had uncovered a compost heap insulated for winter. "You're not playing are you, Fischer? Is there something in there?" He gave a yap in reply.

"Okay! Wait there." She had seen a spade in the shed. At this point there was nothing else for it, if Mrs Duke came out so be it, but whatever Fischer sensed in the compost heap she was going to find it.

The long-handled spade was tall enough to push all the way through to the bottom of the mound. With Fischer clearing the snow on top, all Penny had to do was poke the spade through the straw and leaves to the dense compost below, feeling for anything unusual within. When the spade hit something hard, she began to dig.

"Don't go in the hole, Fischer, we don't know what's

in there and you could be hurt," she warned him. Lifting a mound of compost from the heap, she stared at what she had unearthed. With it's glass glinting in the morning light was a cordial bottle, and next to it a tub of what looked like sugar crystals.

"Oh my..."

Penny let the spade fall to the ground. Pulling her phone out of her pocket with shaking hands, she made a garbled call to DI Monroe before dashing towards the house.

"Quick, Fischer, we have to save Mr Kelly!"

Fischer raced ahead, reaching the back door and scratching at it wildly. Penny, huffing and puffing through the deep snow, caught up and crashed straight in.

"Mr Kelly? Where are you?" She shouted in panic, running through the kitchen into a dark hallway, and slamming open every door she passed. At the last door, she breathed a sigh of relief, "There you are. Thank goodness."

Mr Kelly and Mrs Duke were seated in armchairs either side of the fireplace, a coffee table laden with a tray of refreshments in between. Including a bottle of cordial!

"Penelope Finch! How dare you barge into my home like this? Look at the mess you're making with the snow!" cried Mrs Duke. She placed her hands on the chair arms intending to rise, but Fischer, who had positioned himself in front of her chair, suddenly bared his teeth menacingly and began to growl. Penny had never seen him so vicious. "Control this nasty little dog immediately!" Mrs Duke said, but she lowered herself uncertainly and remained seated.

"He doesn't like you, Mrs Duke. And with good reason. You killed Julia Wargraves."

Suddenly Fischer lunched forward and snapped his teeth, just missing Mrs Duke's ankle, and she pulled her arm away from the fireside. She'd been reaching for the poker.

"I'd sit still if I were you," said Penny. "I know you killed Julia, Mrs Duke. I found the cordial bottle and the cyanide crystals in the compost heap, so there's no point in denying it. Why did you do it?"

Mrs Duke glowered at Penny coldly, "Why do you think, you stupid girl? That nasty, vile woman killed Miss Marmalade! She poisoned her, and my dear, precious kitty died the most horrible death. It was a despicable thing to do, so I gave her a taste of her own medicine. She deserved it and I'd do it again in a heartbeat."

"I'm going to call the police now, Mrs Duke. You'll be arrested for murder," said Mr Kelly, rising form his chair.

"Nonsense. Anyone could have hidden those items in my compost heap. It's my word against yours and who will believe you two meddling fools?"

"I will," said a familiar voice from the door, and Inspector Monroe entered the room.

Penny turned, and Monroe's dancing eyes met hers, causing her heart to soar. He shrugged, "I was already waiting in the village when you called." He inclined his head, indicating they should move to the hallway. "Thank you, Penny, Mr Kelly. Your help has been invaluable. I'll need you to make statements now if that's all right? It would be best to get this on record while it's still fresh in your memories. PC Bolton is outside, I'll get him to collect the bottles from the compost heap when I take Mrs Duke out, then send him in to you."

"Of course," Mr Kelly said.

"Fischer was the hero of the hour," Penny said, feeling inordinately proud of her little dog, who was still taking his guarding duties very seriously. "We couldn't have done it without him. Is it all right if I speak to Susie about this, by the way, I promised her the scoop?"

The Inspector nodded, "Yes, that should be fine. By the time she gets the details Mrs Duke will have been formally charged and locked in a cell. I have to go now, but I'd like to thank you both again, and wish you a very Happy Christmas."

# Eighteen

Christmas dinner at Penny's parents' house was a triumph. The food was glorious and plentiful, crackers had been pulled, silly hats worn and jokes told, and the prizes inside given to Susie's children. Fischer was back to his normal, healthy and excitable self, but was still on his bland diet of rice. However, in honour of it being Christmas, Penny had substituted the chicken with turkey breast.

Now, with the children watching a film in the sitting room next door with Fischer, who, judging from the giggles and exciting barks, was keeping them entertained, the adults could safely discuss the murder. Penny had already brought Susie up to date, and her friend had quickly pulled together a full article for the next edition of the Hampsworthy Gazette. It would appear on the front page, along with Susie's byline. Apparently the editor had been so impressed he'd offered her a part-time junior reporter position on the spot. Penny was thrilled for her friend.

Sheila Finch laid the coffee tray on the table, and helping herself to a mint said, "I can't believe it was Mrs Duke who killed Julia. It beggars belief, it really does. But why did you go there first, Penny? You would have passed Mrs Sykes's house on the way."

"Actually it was because of what Michael from The Rough Spot came and told me. Once he had explained I realised why he was familiar. His girlfriend is Katie Lowry, who works at the Pig and Fiddle. I've seen him waiting at the bar for her to finish her shift. Since the Pig and Fiddle were catering the annual dinner she was working that night, and she sneaked Michael in through the kitchen. He hadn't bought a ticket, which was why he wasn't on the list and never questioned."

"Why didn't he come forward sooner though?" asked Albert, pouring the coffee.

"He didn't realise the importance of what he'd seen until he overheard my conversation with Dr Jones. In fact it wasn't until then that he remembered it all. Apparently he recalled seeing Mrs Duke with a bottle at the party like the one Mrs Wargraves usually carried. The reason he remembered her was because of the way Mrs Duke behaved after her cat died, and how nasty she was about Julia. But even then we didn't really believe she was responsible."

"But you took the bottle from the village hall, Penny. How could you have also found it in Mrs Duke's compost heap?"

"That's a good question, mum. It was simply that Mrs Duke had made too much of the poison and had to use a second bottle. She said she kept it because it might have come in handy, but as soon as it became an official murder inquiry she realised she had to get rid of it. Her idea was to hide it in the compost heap until *the heat had died down*, her actual words would you believe, then she would have ditched it somewhere else where it wouldn't be connected to her."

"She thought it all out didn't she?" said Susie. "But the thing I find most amazing is she added a sedative to the bottle as well."

"What does that do?" asked Albert.

"It would slow down her reaction to the poison," Penny explained, "and stop the foaming at the mouth which Cyanide poisoning can do. It would look like a heart attack initially and she could leave without anyone being the wiser. She researched it all on the Internet apparently."

"That's just awful," said Sheila with a shudder.

"What's worse," said Penny. "Is if it hadn't been for the snow and her inability to get out and hide the poison elsewhere, she'd probably have got away with it."

"Well thank goodness for snow!" said Sheila. "I'm really very proud of you, Penny, and Fischer of course. Albert and I have always said what an intelligent little dog he is."

At the sound of his name, the intelligent little dog came barreling into the kitchen and jumped on Penny's knee.

"Hello little fish face. Did you know we were talking about you?"

"Woof," Came the reply and everyone laughed.

"I must say that was a thoughtful gift from the Inspector," said Sheila, and all eyes turned to the yellow neckerchief Fischer was wearing.

It had paw-prints and the words 'Clever Boy!' embroidered on it in black, and it had brought a tear to Penny's eye when she had opened it. His gift to her had been equally as thoughtful and had made her laugh. It was tucked inside her handbag for later. When she had unwrapped it, Susie had given her a puzzled look, but she'd told her it was just a private joke and her friend had smiled knowingly but kept quiet.

"Would anyone like another piece of Susie's delicious Pavlova?" Penny asked, looking around the table. "Because if there are no takers, Susie and I will clear up and do the dishes. Mum, Dad, go and put your feet up."

"You won't hear any complaints from me," Albert said, rising from his chair.

"Thank you, girls," Sheila said. "I'll put Fischer in his bed too, he's fast asleep there. He's only little and all the excitement has tired him out."

Once they had left, Susie nursed her wine glass and grinned at Penny, "Thanks so much for today. The way you and your parents included us means so much. The kids have had a great time. Here, I got you an extra something.

I thought you could hang it up in the Mystery Mobile."

"Oh, so we're calling it the Mystery Mobile now are we? I feel like I'm on an episode of Scooby Doo!" Penny said with giggles as she unwrapped her gift. "Oh, Susie, it's brilliant. Thank you!" It was a hand crafted wooden sign shaped like an open book, with carved words saying, *'Librarians do it between sheets of paper.'*

"You're welcome. So, do you think Julia really did kill Miss Marmalade?"

Penny sighed and topped up her wineglass, "Honestly? I have no idea. Stanley and Julia were away when the cat was found, but she could have placed it there before she went. Either she poisoned the cat deliberately, poisoned it accidentally, or had nothing to with it all and the cat picked the poison up somewhere else. There's no proof she did anything. But Stanley came out yesterday as we were leaving Mrs Duke's house, and I asked him if Julia used poison in the garden, he said she did. Particularly around the roses."

"Which is where the cat kept doing its business," said Susie.

Penny nodded, "Exactly. But I don't think we'll ever know for sure if Julia deliberately poisoned Miss Marmalade."

"Well let's change the subject, it's Christmas Day, not a time to be talking about murder. So what did Edward get you, you never said?"

Penny grimaced.

"He didn't!"

Penny nodded, "He did. A set of three handkerchiefs with the letter P embroidered on them. Same as last year."

"That man has no imagination."

"It had a three for two sticker on the back."

"Oh, Penny," her friend said sadly.

"I got an extra this year though. A diary. With his accountancy firm's name and address on the front."

Susie stared aghast, "So it was free?"

"Yes, but he'd taken the time to go through it and put in all the important dates. You know, every one of the car club meetings I'm expected to attend with him, and his birthday."

"I'm sorry, Penny. I don't know what to say."

While Susie started on the washing up, Penny took out the book Inspector Monroe had given her and smiled. It was a Seuss classic, Hunches in Bunches.

"You know something, Susie? I actually don't mind. I have a hunch things are going to work out just fine."

## Finch & Fischer will return in —
## **Death at the Duck Pond**

If you would like to be kept up to date with new releases and receive **The Yellow Cottage Mystery** (The prequel short story to the Yellow Cottage Vintage Mysteries) for free, please sign up to my **Readers Group mailing list** on the website: **www.jnewwrites.com.**

If you enjoyed *Death at the Duck Pond*, please consider leaving a review online at **Amazon.**

Connect with J. New online:

**BOOKBUB**

https://www.bookbub.com/authors/j-new

**FACEBOOK**

https://www.facebook.com/jnewwrites

**TWITTER**

https://twitter.com/newwrites

**GOODREADS**

http://www.goodreads.com/author/show/7984711.J_New

**WEBSITE**

https://www.jnewwrites.com/

Made in the USA
Columbia, SC
27 February 2022